He opened the door to the May day, expecting to see a friend.

When he saw Brenna McDougall, his heart skipped at least one beat and his chest tightened.

Suddenly he realized she wasn't alone. She was carrying a baby!

Riley's military training served him well as he stood straight and stoic while his head spun and he calculated the fact that the infant looked to be about six-weeks old. Six-weeks old.

Keep your head on straight. Listen to her before you make a giant leap to the wrong conclusion.

"Hi, Riley," Brenna said brightly. Then her confidence seemed to fade. "Maybe I should have called first, but I thought this was the best way to do it."

"Do what?" He was proud his voice remained even as he remembered their fifteen-year high school reunion, their passionate night in his bed, then her departure without a word or a goodbye or a note.

"I had a baby. Derek is…your son."

Dear Reader,

A man and a baby.

What can draw out a man's tender side more completely than his child? I remember when our son was around three, my husband took him for a walk in our backyard. They crouched beside a rosebush and my husband let him smell the rose. I even shot a photo of it. It's a tender moment I'll always remember.

As a former marine, my hero, Riley, is usually a tough guy. But his stirred-up feelings for Brenna and his infant son change him. I hope you enjoy reading about his journey into fatherhood and his realization that since high school, Brenna has been the love of his life.

All my best,

Karen Rose Smith

RILEY'S BABY BOY

KAREN ROSE SMITH

ISBN-13: 978-0-373-65687-5

RILEY'S BABY BOY

This edition published by arrangement with Harlequin Books S.A.

For questions and comments about the quality of this book please contact us at Customer_eCare@Harlequin.ca.

www.Harlequin.com

Printed in U.S.A.

Books by Karen Rose Smith

Harlequin Special Edition

‡‡_His Country Cinderella_ #2137
**_Once Upon a Groom_ #2146
**_The CEO's Unexpected Proposal_ #2201
**_Riley's Baby Boy_ #2205

Silhouette Special Edition

Abigail and Mistletoe #930
The Sheriff's Proposal #1074
His Little Girl's Laughter #1426
Expecting the CEO's Baby #1535
Their Baby Bond #1588
Take a Chance on Me #1599
Which Child Is Mine? #1655
¤_Cabin Fever_ #1682
§§_Custody for Two_ #1753
§§_The Baby Trail_ #1767
§§_Expecting His Brother's Baby_ #1779
†_The Super Mom_ #1797
††_Falling for the Texas Tycoon_ #1807
~_The Daddy Dilemma_ #1884
§_Her Mr. Right?_ #1897
~_The Daddy Plan_ #1908
~_The Daddy Verdict_ #1925
*_Lullaby for Two_ #1961
*_The Midwife's Glass Slipper_ #1972
~~_The Texas Bodyguard's Proposal_ #1987
*_Baby by Surprise_ #1997
*_The Texas Billionaire's Baby_ #2032
*_The Texan's Happily-Ever-After_ #2044
‡_From Doctor…To Daddy_ #2065
*_Twins under His Tree_ #2087
**_His Daughter…Their Child_ #2098

Silhouette Books

The Fortunes of Texas
Marry in Haste…

Logan's Legacy
A Precious Gift

The Fortunes of Texas: Reunion
The Good Doctor

Signature Select

Secret Admirer
"Dream Marriage"

§§Baby Bonds
¤Montana Mavericks:
Gold Rush Grooms
†Talk of the Neighborhood
††Logan's Legacy Revisited
§The Wilder Family
~Dads in Progress
*The Baby Experts
~~The Foleys and the McCords
‡Montana Mavericks:
Thunder Canyon Cowboys
**Reunion Brides
‡‡Montana Mavericks:
The Texans are Coming!

Other titles by this author available in ebook format.

KAREN ROSE SMITH

is the award-winning, bestselling novelist of seventy-nine published romances. Her latest series, The Reunion Brides, is set near Flagstaff, Arizona, in Miners Bluff, the fictional town she created. After visiting Flagstaff, the Grand Canyon and Sedona, the scenery was so awe-inspiring that she knew she had to set books there. When not writing, she likes to garden, growing herbs, vegetables and flowers. She lives with her husband—her college sweetheart—and their two cats in Pennsylvania. Readers may email her through her website, www.karenrosesmith.com, follow her on Facebook or Twitter @karenrosesmith or write to her at P.O. Box 1545, Hanover, PA 17331.

To DeSales Sterner—
a wonderful mother, grandmother, sister and friend.
We love you.

Chapter One

The first knock on Riley O'Rourke's door was hesitant.

The second was stronger.

Riley opened the door to the May day, expecting to see a friend. Family never knocked when they visited his house in the woods. They barged in. However, when he saw Brenna McDougall, his heart skipped at least one beat and his chest tightened because…

She was holding a baby!

Riley's marine training was the only thing keeping him standing while his head spun. The infant looked to be about six weeks old. Six weeks old.

Keep your head on straight. Listen to her before you make a giant leap to the wrong conclusion.

"Hi, Riley," Brenna said brightly. Then her confidence seemed to fade. "Maybe I should have called first, but I thought this was the best way to do it."

"Do what?" He was proud his voice remained even

as he remembered their fifteenth-year high school reunion, their passionate night in his bed, then her departure without a word or a goodbye or a note.

"I had a baby. Derek is…your son."

Seeing Brenna again had knocked him for a loop, but her statement of his paternity felt like a sucker punch.

A former marine, he never lost his composure—not in the field, not in his post-military life. Raking his fingers through the black hair that had grown out over the past year, he recovered quickly. Yet he couldn't take his gaze off of the little boy in Brenna's arms.

"I guess you'd better come in," he said, wishing he'd taken a shower, wishing he and Brenna didn't have a past between them full of regrets.

Brenna held on to Derek as if he was the most precious bundle on earth. She rubbed her cheek against the baby's and murmured something soft…something Riley didn't understand.

"He's just waking up," she explained. "He was so good on the plane. And he fell asleep again on the drive from Flagstaff to Miners Bluff. I came straight here."

Another surprise. Why hadn't she driven to her parents' first? After all, Brenna was the obedient, loyal daughter. Okay. He was still cynical about that.

Although she'd been in his house the night of their reunion last summer, her gaze wandered over it as if she were seeing it for the first time. One word could describe his place—comfortable. After living in the desert, in barracks, huts and bunkers, he'd wanted comfortable as well as enough furniture to seat a good portion of his family. With his dad, two brothers and a sister who sometimes dropped in unexpectedly, he needed a place for them to land.

With Derek in her arms Brenna turned around, assessing the long sofa and Western-patterned earth tones, the native-stone hearth, the recliner. There were two cushy chairs angled to watch the large-screen TV. Outside the dining area's sliding glass doors, she could glimpse a patio with its brick wall and outdoor fireplace.

Still, Riley wasn't concerned about her opinion of his house.

Anger created a slow burn through his blood. "Why didn't you tell me you were pregnant?"

When she looked up at him with her sea-green eyes and pushed her long blond hair over her shoulder in a nervous gesture that had been a habit since high school, he almost forgot to listen.

"It's complicated."

"It's complicated?" he snapped. When he realized his voice was a little too rough with a baby present, even though that baby had *his* blue eyes, he vowed to stay calm.

His gruffness didn't seem to intimidate Brenna. After she stole a glance at him, she went to sit on the long sofa, settling the baby, who was dressed in a blue-and-white-striped onesie, in the crook of her arm. Derek waved his arms and smiled, if a six-week-old could smile. Brenna obviously thought he could because she smiled back and tickled his tummy.

But her smile slid away as her gaze met Riley's. "I couldn't get back to Miners Bluff before now."

"Cell phone service might be a little spotty out here, but I do have a landline. I'm listed in the Miners Bluff directory."

She ran her thumb over the embroidered puppy on Derek's outfit. "I needed time, Riley, to figure out what I wanted to do. I was in the middle of designing a new bridal gown collection. I had orders for custom gowns. I had a show in March and then I went into labor early—"

He crossed his arms over his chest. "So?"

"So…I just didn't know how I was going to handle all of it…any of it…*you*."

"You wanted to *handle* me?"

Now her temper flared. "You *know* what I mean. I live in New York. You live here. I didn't know how you'd feel about me being pregnant. It wasn't as if we…we…"

"Picked up where we left off the summer after high school?"

"The night of the reunion, we knew we were having a fling for old times' sake."

Old times' sake. She'd hit *that* nail on its proverbial head.

The night of the reunion they'd fallen into the past and hadn't cared about the future. But now here she was, sitting on his sofa with his son.

His son.

Some of the shock was wearing off now, and as he approached the sofa and sat beside Brenna, the scent of her perfume, the curves of her body, the glossiness of her blond hair aroused him, just as they had when they'd danced the night of the reunion.

He steeled himself against the attraction that had begun when they were teenagers. "Can I hold him?"

Her eyes widened as if she hadn't expected that. A reluctance seemed to come over her and he wondered what that was about. If he didn't put her at ease, she could walk out that door and fly back to New York.

"I won't drop him," he said, with his own attempt at a smile, although it didn't come easy. "Whenever I was home on leave, I handled my brothers' and sister's kids."

Brenna smoothed Derek's wavy black hair, then lifted him, warning, "You have to support his head."

"I know."

Those two words, *I know,* had an underlying message. As their gazes met, video flashed through his mind of himself and Brenna exploring each other. Their cravings when they were teenagers had defied their families' hostility. Rebellion and defiance at work?

How stupid they'd been as teenagers. How reckless as adults.

As he took his son into his arms, Riley's heart almost stopped. A protective urge he'd never felt before washed over him as he supported Derek's head and then cradled his son in his arms.

He was a father!

Or *was* he? He had to ask the question, especially since Brenna had said she'd gone into labor early.

"Are you sure he's mine?"

There was a look on Brenna's face that he couldn't decipher. He wasn't sure if it was indignation or hurt. When she blinked, it disappeared and she lifted her chin. He knew *that* gesture. She was going to defend herself for all she was worth.

"I gave birth to Derek two weeks before my due date. I haven't slept with anyone but you for a very long time."

A very long time. Exactly what did she mean by that? Months? A year? Two? And why not? Brenna was even more beautiful now than she'd been in high school, with long golden hair, green eyes, a face that could have rivaled Helen of Troy's. Oh, Lord, he was turning poetic. Brenna had always done that to him and he'd felt like a fool because of it. Yet as he sat next to her, realized her breasts were a little fuller, her hips a little rounder, an instinctive primal reaction he'd always had to her threatened to override any good thoughts or sense.

"But if you want a DNA test, no problem." She glanced at him again and then added, "Maybe you don't want a DNA test. Maybe you don't want any part of..." She took a breath then motioned to her son. "Derek."

Brenna had come from money, was beautiful, intelligent and always self-assured. But today there was an air of uncertainty about her. Because she hadn't known what his reaction would be?

"I haven't heard the roof blow off your parents' house. Did you tell them who you think the father is?"

"I don't *think*. I *know*." She reached over and touched Derek's little hand. Her arm grazed his and the awareness between them was instantaneous and potent, as it had been from the beginning.

His gaze drifted from her eyes to the pulse at her throat and it was fluttering rapidly. So was his. He waited.

"They don't know about Derek."

Riley felt suddenly confused. "They don't know he's a boy? They don't know you've had him? They don't know I'm the father?"

"All of the above." Her voice faltered and he saw that she was tired from the trip and filled with anxiety.

"You didn't tell them you were pregnant? How could they not know? Didn't you see them at Christmas?" After all, the McDougalls were a close-knit family. They celebrated holidays. They kept traditions. They did everything right. Except Angus McDougall wasn't always so right when it came to business.

"I didn't really start showing until my sixth month. When they came to New York for Christmas, I wore heavy sweaters. They didn't notice and I didn't let on."

"Because?" he prompted.

"Because I didn't want any interference. When I left Miners Bluff, it was for a reason. You know that. I had trunk shows planned for winter and a collection to get out."

"Trunk shows?"

He hadn't been able to keep the real amusement from his voice. She gave in and shot him a half-smile. That smile was like a kick to the gut.

"I bring other designers' gowns into my store and they show mine. It's a great sales tool."

She'd learned all about sales from wandering after her father in his department store downtown. The idea of that department store and of what Angus McDougall had done to his father could always make Riley see red.

As if Brenna knew that and didn't want to get in to it, she hurried on. "I wasn't sure what I was going to do, if I was going to come back here."

"If you were going to tell me?"

Derek suddenly became restless, fretful, and Riley knew his son had probably caught that edge of anger in his voice. Careful once again to support the baby's head, Riley picked him up, his hand practically spanning from Derek's hair to midway down his back. He spoke to him softly and then nestled him in his arm once again. The baby quieted under his care.

"You're good with him." Brenna seemed really surprised.

"Brenna, you're going to have to start trusting me." He saw the look in her eyes that said she didn't, the look that told him old insecurities die hard. She'd never really known if he'd dated her and bedded her in high school to get revenge on her father. It might have started that way, but in the end, he'd been tied up in knots over her.

And what had she done? She'd been loyal to her family and she'd left.

How could they ever raise a child together when they didn't trust each other?

"Trust goes two ways, Riley," she said. "We'll get that DNA test."

"I know a good pediatrician my sister uses. I can probably make an appointment for tomorrow."

"Next day maybe?"

He was about to make a comment about postponing the inevitable when she held up her hand. "I don't think I can face my parents tonight. I called The Purple Pansy Bed and Breakfast and Mikala's aunt, Anna Conti, has a suite free. I'm going to take Derek there for tonight. I'll go to see my parents in the morning." Mikala had been one of their high school classmates.

"Wait a minute." Riley held the baby a little tighter. "You just got here. I don't know how long you're going to stay, and I deserve a chance to be with my son. You don't even have the supplies you need, do you? Diapers? Formula?"

"I packed enough diapers and I'm breastfeeding. I do have some formula, too. I came prepared."

Brenna was that type, usually always prepared. He could see how that would be a good trait as a mom. "All right, so you have what you need. But I need time with him. Stay here tonight until we figure things out."

She went completely still and he could see she was trying to gauge his level of sincerity. "You want to change diapers, too?"

"That's part of being a dad, isn't it?"

"It is, though a part a lot of parents like to skip."

"Some parents skip out altogether. We both know that. That's not going to happen here." There was a very good reason he didn't trust women. His mother had left Miners Bluff for the "good" life. Essentially Brenna had done the same. She wouldn't go public with what they'd felt when they were young. She wouldn't defy her parents and admit her feelings about him. She'd felt leaving was better than staying. He wondered if she knew that's what had eventually led to him joining the marines.

This time, without any hesitation at all, she reached over and touched his thigh. Her fingers on his skin were a searing heat. "Riley, I didn't mean to suggest—"

To his relief, Derek started fussing again. This time he was grateful and didn't croon or rock. He wasn't going to revisit his broken-up family life with Brenna. He wasn't going to let her touch turn him inside out.

When she reached for Derek, Riley let her lift the baby from his arms to walk with him.

He was gripped by longing he didn't begin to understand. He rose to his feet and with his best military voice, asked, "So will you stay here tonight? Stay here while you're in Miners Bluff?"

Brenna seemed to weigh all of her options. Finally she responded, "I'll stay tonight, then we'll go from there."

One night. He had one night to convince her he could be a proper father...one night to convince her he wasn't and would *never* be like his dad.

Brenna had just finished fastening Derek's diaper, when a tingle ran up her spine. Keeping one hand on Derek, she glanced over her shoulder and there was Riley, all tall and brawny and broad-shouldered...watching her. She felt hotter than she should have for May in Miners Bluff.

He came into the room and she saw he was carrying what looked to be a dresser drawer.

"What's that?" She was still nervous about coming, still uncertain she'd done the right thing. The bad feelings between her family and Riley's had caused their breakup in the past and could complicate their decisions now.

"Derek needs a bed. You can't just put him beside you and roll over on him."

"I would never—" She stopped, seeing the glint of humor in Riley's eyes. He was trying to lighten the situation and she really did appreciate that. Why she was questioning her decision to come here, she didn't know. Her life had been full of decisions. Leaving Riley had been heartbreaking, but it had been the right decision. Her career had been solid. One bad decision still haunted her, though. She'd become romantically involved with the wrong man—Thad Johnson—and had ended up emotionally bruised. But Thad had taught her men couldn't be trusted…not any more than Riley, whose motives had always been in question.

"For a bed, it's kind of hard, don't you think?" she asked, trying to forget the past…at least, for the moment.

"Oh ye of little faith," Riley said with a shake of his head. "Just watch."

When he exited the room again, she watched all right. She watched the straightness of his spine and the play of his muscles under his T-shirt. His jeans fit him *really* well. She knew what he looked like without those jeans. That was the problem with staying here.

By the time she'd scooped Derek off the bed, Riley had returned with an armful of linens. First he took what looked like a mattress pad and folded it in half. Next he tucked a sheet around it and smoothed it out in the drawer, ensuring the surface was tight.

"What do you think?"

With Derek on her shoulder, she crossed to his side of the bed and stood next to him. Way too close, she decided, but that's where the drawer was so she had no choice.

She pushed down on the makeshift mattress. "You're inventive."

"I was a marine."

He hadn't said much about being in the service, but at the reunion, she'd heard chatter before he'd arrived about his tours of duty, about his Purple Heart and Bronze Star. As they'd danced he'd explained about how he'd become Clay Sullivan's partner in his wilderness guided tour business, about how he was glad to be home with his family. But their conversation hadn't delved deeper than the surface of their lives. His dad had been an alcoholic. Had that changed?

She'd never really gotten to know Riley's brothers and sister because their high school affair had been a secret. That summer after their high school graduation, Riley had wanted to go public with their relationship. But her dad and Riley's dad had felt nothing but bitterness toward each other. She'd been torn by her feelings for Riley and her desire to leave Miners Bluff and become the independent woman she wanted to be—by her sense of loyalty to her family and her love for Riley.

Family and independence had won and she'd gone to the Fashion Institute of Technology in New York with her heart aching, her appetite gone, her nights filled with dreams of Riley and what they'd had. Yet she doubted what they'd had, too. Had Riley really fallen for her? Or had he just wanted revenge on her father for what *her* father had done to *his?*

"Did you learn to cook in the marines?" He'd made them a quick supper of grilled burgers, oven fries and fresh green beans.

"I learned almost everything I know as an adult in the marines."

That sentence carried a lot of weight and she wasn't going to ignore its importance. She patted Derek's back as she rocked back and forth a little, more for her sake than his.

"When did you enlist?"

"The November after we graduated."

"What made you decide? You'd never mentioned wanting to serve."

He smoothed the padding in the drawer again, straightened, looking uneasy. "It's not important."

"It changed the course of your life and made you who you are. I think it is."

"I got into trouble."

That wouldn't have been the first time Riley had been in trouble. Before she'd met him, before she'd dated him, she'd known he was wild. Liam O'Rourke's kids had never had restrictions, and Riley had taken advantage of that. Sure, after his mom had left, he'd had to help with his brothers and his sister. But when he wasn't doing that, he was raising Cain. She'd been told to stay away from him for more than one reason. But this raven-haired bad boy, with eyes as blue as the winter sky, had been temptation personified when he'd seemed interested in her.

He and some friends had been caught stealing another school's mascot. He'd also been caught binge drinking with those same buddies in a neighbor's barn.

"This time it was worse than school suspension," he admitted finally, guessing what she was thinking. "I had a few beers. I drove Dad's truck and crashed it into a fire hydrant."

He'd had no plans for the future when they'd dated. He'd had no goals as she'd had. "What happened?"

"My case was assigned to a judge who did more than look at me as a number. He told me to shape up or die young. He advised me to visit the offices of recruiters. He told me if they accepted me and I signed up, he'd forget the fire hydrant and the damages. So I signed up."

"You were a marine until last year?"

"Until a few months before the reunion. Since I'm skilled at computer intel, I did consulting work when I got back. But I was looking for something different. When I heard Clay was searching for a partner, guiding work seemed perfect. And it is. I know this area as well as he does and my training just adds skills that I can use when I take tours fishing or riding out to Horsethief Canyon or rock climbing near Sedona. The marines made me a man of many talents."

"I don't think it was just the marines. You must have been willing to learn."

Their gazes connected and something like old feelings zipped between them. Not only old feelings—an attraction that had lasted over fifteen years. How could that possibly be?

"What time do you turn in?" he asked, his voice gruff.

"Soon. I'm beat. Traveling with a little one can be a bit exhausting." She gave Derek a tiny kiss on his ear. "I didn't know what I was going to do if he'd cried on the plane. But he only fussed a little and no one seemed to mind. There's just so much paraphernalia to bring along with a baby."

Riley glanced at the stack of diapers tipping out of her suitcase, at the box of powdered formula on her dresser, at all the little outfits and booties that were toppling over on the bedroom chair.

"Did you fit in any of *your* clothes?"

She laughed. "A few. I figured I could pick up something here. It was more important I had everything I needed for Derek, just in case I got stuck in an airport or stalled in a car or something. Being a mom has changed the way I think about *everything*."

She saw the questions in Riley's eyes but she didn't have any answers.

He must have known that because he hefted up the drawer, took it to the side of the bed nearest the wall and set it on the floor. "Is that going to be all right?"

"It will be fine. He'll sleep for me in his car seat, but this is good until I can buy a portable crib tomorrow."

"I have a bath attached to my bedroom so feel free to use the hall bathroom. It has a shower."

"I know."

His cheeks grew a little ruddy and she knew he was just making conversation, trying to dispel awkwardness between them. But it was there and nothing they could say would change that. They'd broken up as teenagers, had a one night stand as adults, and now here they were…with a baby. How much more awkward could it get?

She knew she shouldn't ask.

Suddenly more tired from the long day than she'd wanted to admit, she sank down onto the bed holding her son close.

Abruptly Riley said, "I'm going out for a run."

"In the dark?"

"I was a marine," he said again.

She suspected he just didn't want to be in the house with her. "I'll see you in the morning then. I'm going to drive to my parents' after breakfast."

He was silent for a few moments, then offered, "If you need anything during the night…for the baby—" He added quickly, "Just give a yell. I'm a light sleeper."

A light sleeper? He hadn't awakened the night of the reunion when she'd slipped out of his bed, dressed and driven away. But she didn't bring that up. She didn't ask him why he'd slept so soundly after they'd made love.

But they hadn't made love. They'd had sex, and she'd better remember that.

When Riley left the room, she closed her eyes and held her baby even closer.

Chapter Two

Brenna shouldn't be nervous. She really shouldn't. After all, these were her parents. They'd loved her, given her anything they could and protected her. She and her dad had a particularly special bond for reasons she'd never confided in Riley. When she was little, her dad had literally saved her life. However, she'd run from her parents' protection to find out if she could stand on her own. Now here she was, with Riley beside her, standing at their door, hoping her father didn't blow a gasket.

"Are you sure you want to come in with me? You don't have to," she told him.

"Brenna, this is my son. I'm not going to let your father dictate what's going to happen next."

"Do you think I can't stand up to him?"

Riley just gave her a look that said it all. She hadn't before. She'd forgotten about him and what they'd had in order to be loyal to her family. Maybe if she'd revealed the reasons for some of that loyalty... But she'd been afraid he wouldn't understand so she'd kept those thoughts and feelings to herself. She hadn't wanted to give him ammunition he could use to hurt her or her dad.

She snuggled Derek close to her shoulder, not wanting him to be a pawn, not wanting anything negative ever to touch him. In that moment, she realized why her parents had so fiercely wanted to protect *her*.

Riley had insisted on coming along and she'd let him. He had rights, too, and maybe she *was* afraid her father would steamroll her. He'd done it all her life until she'd decided to leave.

"Can you promise me you won't lose your temper?" she asked, worried. Riley's bitterness toward her father had never ebbed. She could see it in his eyes and hear it in his voice. It was simple, really. Her father had made a decision that had cost Liam O'Rourke his restaurant, his wife and his sobriety. But in defense of her father, he'd made a *business* decision. Rumors Liam had spread about her dad afterward had damaged her dad's reputation. It had been an ugly situation for both families.

Brenna realized no one understood her father as she and her mother did. She knew details about his childhood her parents had never wanted her to know. She'd been about twelve when she'd overheard a conversation about how her dad's own father had physically abused him. Maybe that's one of the reasons her dad had always tried to give her the best life possible...had showered her with every advantage he could manage.

When the gray-haired housekeeper who had been handling household details for the past twenty-five years opened the door and saw Brenna, she burst into a grin. "Miss Brenna! How wonderful to see you. And who's this you're holding?"

Then Miriam caught sight of Riley just a step behind her. Her mouth rounded in a huge O as she recognized him.

"Are my parents home?" Since it was early, she was hoping her father hadn't left for the department store yet, or her mother for errands.

"Your parents are having breakfast. Are they expecting you?" Miriam again gave Riley a look up and down as if surprised by the idea they might be. The McDougalls didn't associate with the O'Rourkes.

"Actually, this is a surprise," Brenna responded with high energy. "We're just going to go right in. You don't have to announce us."

Before Miriam could object, Brenna glanced over her shoulder at Riley for the go-ahead, passed the housekeeper, strolled through the beautiful marble-floored foyer and into the dining room where her father had a paper propped in front of his face. Her mother was sipping a cup of coffee catty-corner from him at the mahogany dining room table.

Brenna's mother looked up when she heard footsteps, but her father kept his eyes on his newspaper. Her mother's green eyes, so like Brenna's own, rounded in astonishment. She was a tall, slim woman with ash-blond hair that she kept perfectly maintained. Her makeup was always impeccable, too, but now her astonishment caused wrinkles on her forehead and around her eyes as she quickly pushed back her chair and hurried around the table.

"Oh my gosh, Brenna. Why didn't you *tell* us you were coming? And who's this little one?" Then she looked up at Riley. "And why is *he* here?"

Brenna transferred Derek to Riley to give her mother a hug. Her father folded his paper, laid it on the table and glanced up. His gaze first targeted Riley…then the baby…then Brenna. He slowly and stiffly stood, assessing the situation.

"You always call before you come," he said gruffly. "You've never brought a baby before and you certainly never brought *him*. What's going on, Brenna?"

A chill went up Brenna's spine at the disapproval in her father's voice. She felt her cheeks flush and she wanted to grab for Derek again. But she knew her son was better off in Riley's arms. It made a point. It made a statement—one that her father obviously understood even before she explained.

"I didn't call first because I wasn't sure exactly when I could get away. I also wanted to tell you my news in person, not over the phone." She reached for Derek again and Riley transferred the baby back to her. When she brushed her finger along his cheek, she was filled with that overwhelming love that had to spill over.

Her eyes met Riley's and she almost shook from the charge that ran through her body. They had intimate knowledge of each other and that was potent. Then she turned to face her parents.

"Mom and Dad, this is your grandson, Derek. Riley is his father."

Her mother gasped. Her father seemed to freeze before her eyes. His battle with hair loss had been going on for years. He was shorter than Riley, about five-ten, but he was husky and Brenna had always felt safe when he hugged her. She'd always felt safe because he could protect her. She'd always felt safe because he would give his life for her and she knew it.

Mainly, Riley didn't know the story behind that because they'd tried to *not* discuss their parents.

"Oh my," her mother said weakly, as if it were all too

much for her. But then she rallied. "Why don't we go into the living room and talk. Unless you'd like some breakfast? Miriam could make you scrambled eggs, toast, pancakes, anything you'd like." She couldn't seem to take her gaze from Derek.

Her father was still frozen, but his face was turning red.

"We ate before we came," Brenna responded to keep the conversation going. "Derek had us up early, so we went with his schedule."

Afraid her father might have a coronary, she watched him closely. He blew out a draft of air and his color receded a bit. His voice was steely when he said, "I can't believe you didn't tell us you were pregnant. And to bring *him* here. You know how we feel about him and his family. You're flaunting it in our face. What were you thinking?"

Brenna's throat grew thick as she saw the disappointment and betrayal on her father's face.

Her dad picked up steam and his voice grew louder. "Babies change your life. This one's surely going to change yours. How do you expect to keep the hours you do, the nonstop schedule, the traveling for the custom appointments? Are you going to tell me this was planned, Brenna? Did you and…" He stopped a moment, "Did you and O'Rourke *want* this to happen? Out of anybody in the whole world you could have chosen to have a baby with, I don't understand why you chose *him*."

This meeting would set the tone for everything that would happen from now on between her, Riley and her parents. And Derek would be in the thick of it. She had to stand her ground and somehow convince her parents that she knew what was best for their grandson or there would be constant bickering and arguing and her dad would try to cut Riley out of Derek's life.

When Riley took a step closer to her as if to support her effort, she bumped her elbow against his for the contact. "Dad, isn't it time you put any hard feelings you have to rest? What happened years ago shouldn't still keep affecting us now. Can't we move on?"

"What do you want to move on *to,* Brenna? O'Rourke?" Her father snorted as if that idea was beneath them all. He shook his head. "Why didn't you tell us about your pregnancy at Christmas when we came to New York?"

Just why hadn't she? "Riley didn't know yet. I didn't think it was right that you knew if he didn't. I also needed time to get used to the idea of being pregnant, to figure out how it fit in with my career, to decide whether I wanted to move back to Miners Bluff."

At that bit of news Riley gave her a sharp glance.

She quickly went on. "I decided I don't want to move back here. My life is in New York now—my business, my friends, everything. That's where I want to raise Derek. I knew you'd want to convince me to come back. I suspected Riley would, too. I had to be able to withstand the pressure and know exactly what I wanted. So I waited."

Her father wasn't pleased with *that* explanation. His scowl cut even deeper. "So exactly *why* are you here, Brenna? To tell us you had a baby and you're going back to New York?"

She stepped closer to her father. "Daddy, I'm here to introduce you to your grandson. I want to stay awhile so you can get to know each other. And the same is true for Riley. He deserved to meet his son."

Looking as if he wanted to argue with her, her dad

obviously wasn't giving Riley any standing…in his mind or in his house.

"Do you have your things with you?" he asked curtly. "We can move you into your old room, pull out your old cradle. You can have everything you need—"

"Mr. McDougall, that's *not* going to happen."

For the first time Riley broke the silence and Brenna heard the hard determination in his voice. His military demeanor was obvious in the straightness of his posture. He didn't look ruffled or disturbed. He was just standing firm.

"What do you mean that's not going to happen?" her dad demanded hotly. "She's *my* daughter. This is *my* grandson. She needs a place where she'll be comfortable and have everything she needs. This is her home."

Brenna's mom came up beside him and put her hand on his arm. He went quiet.

Riley didn't raise his voice. He didn't have to. Everything about him shouted controlled power. "What you say is true. Brenna and Derek need to be comfortable and have what they need. They will at my house. I'd like Brenna to stay with me while she's here. We have a lot to settle. Under the same roof we can't ignore the important questions. I'm going to get to know Derek and take care of him the way a father should."

Brenna's mother intervened in the highly charged atmosphere. "Brenna, what do you want to do? Stay with Riley? Or stay with us?"

Caught off guard by the question, Brenna knew she had to do what was best for Derek.

"Derek needs to know his dad, and Riley and I have details to iron out on how we're going to manage parenting from two different sides of the country."

When her father began to protest, she assured him,

"Don't worry, Daddy. I promise you'll get to see Derek while I'm here. I rented a car and you're only ten minutes away from Riley's. I'm going to be working while I'm in Miners Bluff, but I'll make sure you can see Derek as often as you want. I know this is a huge shock, but I hope a happy shock. I love this little boy with all my heart. I'm going to always try to do what's best for him like you did for me." Her gaze met her dad's and held. "So if I make a decision you don't agree with, please try to keep that in mind."

"You made a decision I don't agree with, all right," her father muttered. "Just when did this happen?"

"Daddy!" Brenna was shocked that he'd ask this way.

"Angus, that's none of our business," his wife murmured.

"It was the night of the reunion, wasn't it?" her dad decided. "You two got tangled up in talking about the past and—"

Riley cut in. "Mr. McDougall, what happened between Brenna and me is *our* business, not yours."

Brenna had been about to say something like that, only not exactly in that way. Maybe not as bluntly. But she could easily see Riley wasn't going to back down. She admired that but she also knew his attitude would make everything harder. She knew how to negotiate with her dad. Riley didn't.

Brenna's mom must have sensed the same thing because she came over to her daughter and broke the direction of the conversation. "Can I hold him?"

"Of course you can hold him."

Her mother took Derek and gazed down at him with a grandmother's love. "I guess you wouldn't think about leaving him with us now."

"I just got in last evening, Mom. Riley wants to spend

some time with him and we also have to shop and buy supplies for him while I'm here. I'm breastfeeding for now so it's better if Derek stays with me."

Her mother looked deflated.

"I'm going to try using a bottle with him soon, though. I promise, I'll bring him over for a few hours after we're settled in."

After her mother held Derek a few more minutes, she reluctantly handed him back. "Are you sure you can't stay for breakfast…or something?"

"I think it's better if we leave now, Mom."

After a few more minutes of small talk where Riley became remote and her dad scowled, her mother said, "I'll walk you to the door."

Riley walked a few paces ahead.

Brenna's mother came up to her left shoulder and said in a low voice, "Don't hesitate to come back here if anything gets too hard. Some men don't like babies around. Riley can think he wants to be a dad, but doing it is something else. This is your home, honey. Always remember that."

"I will."

She was sure Riley had overheard her mom.

Once outside he turned to her. "I'm going to be a dad, Brenna. Don't doubt that. Whatever I don't know how to do, I'll learn. And as far as liking having babies around, I like my son already. That won't be a problem."

"Riley, she just wants me to know—"

"That you can come running home. I get that. I get it all too well."

Then he walked to the SUV and opened the back door, ready to put Derek in his car seat. Brenna guessed he was ready to do whatever was necessary to claim his son. That scared her.

* * *

When they returned to Riley's house, Brenna was rattled. She concentrated on Derek—changing him, feeding him, rocking him to sleep. Riley didn't peek his head in to find out what she was doing. She heard him on the phone, though, his deep baritone carrying as he made an appointment for their DNA test the following day.

She knew why she felt shaken up. It was starting all over again, that torn-apart feeling. She loved her parents and they loved her, and she'd always tried to be the loyal daughter. She'd given up Riley back then, partly because of them, partly because she hadn't known what to do. Now she understood that they wanted to spend time with their grandson, which was only natural. She wanted them to. She'd like nothing better than to have one big happy family. But she could still see the bitterness and resentment in Riley's eyes when he looked at her dad, his standoffishness toward her mom. She could easily see her parents' reaction to Riley, even though they didn't know the man he'd become.

And here she was, staying in enemy camp.

With Derek asleep, Brenna went to look for Riley. They had to buy supplies. She found him in the kitchen, standing in front of the open refrigerator peering inside. Actually he seemed to be staring into space, but what did she know?

"Is he asleep?" Riley asked, closing the door without pulling anything out.

"Yes, he is. He's really such a good baby."

"I didn't know if you needed help, but I didn't want to disturb you."

Did that mean he didn't want to see her breastfeeding?

"You wouldn't have disturbed us. Thanks for thinking about my need for privacy, but I don't mind if you see. I mean, I cover up."

The nerve in Riley's jaw worked. She wondered what he was thinking, but she didn't find out because he raked his hand through his hair and asked, "Grilled cheese sandwiches for lunch?"

"Grilled cheese is fine. I think I saw some carrots in there. That will take care of my vegetable. I'm going to need to go shopping this afternoon for everything I need for Derek."

He eyed her with sudden intense concentration. "Do you want to do that alone, or do you want me to come along?"

"You're welcome to come along."

"That's not what I asked. Do you *want* me to come along?"

Nothing had ever been easy between them. "If I buy a crib, I could probably use your help to get it in and out of my car. Handling Derek along with supplies—"

Suddenly Riley was there, right in front of her, close enough to touch. "Do you want me to come along?" he drawled slowly. "Anyone can lift a crib in and out of a car. I'm sure the store would be glad to have someone carry everything for you, especially if you go to McDougall's."

Of course she would go to McDougall's for the crib. That was one reason she thought Riley might opt out of this.

"Do you want to set foot in McDougall's?"

Riley blew out a breath. "No, I don't want to set foot in McDougall's. My family has gone the whole way to Flagstaff to avoid buying anything from your father's store. But I will go there to pick out a crib for my son, or anything else he needs. And I want to make something clear, Brenna. I'm paying for it."

"Riley—"

He clasped her shoulders and looked deep into her eyes. "I will provide for him, especially when we're buying things he's going to use in my house. So don't argue with me."

This was the Riley she'd known in high school, the stubborn, sometimes defiant, boy who was determined to get his own way. She had to choose her battles carefully. She knew pride was as important to the O'Rourkes as it was to the McDougalls.

"If you want to pay for the crib, that's fine. But I'll pay for the diapers and—"

As his hand left her shoulder and came up to stroke her hair away from her face, she lost every thought in her head. No man's touch had ever affected her the way Riley's had. His blue eyes didn't waver from hers… didn't give her any room for escape.

"Having you under my roof is damn difficult," he muttered. "I remember the last time you were here, our clothes scattered on the living room floor, down the hall to the bedroom. I remember the way you wrapped your arms and legs around me—"

"Riley…" She wasn't sure if saying his name was meant to warn him or encourage him. He must have taken it as encouragement because suddenly his hands slipped under her hair. Then he was holding her still, bending his head, kissing her hard.

Nothing about Riley O'Rourke was soft—not his attitude, not his sense of purpose, not the muscles in his shoulders or in his arms or in the rest of his body. Riley defined the word *male* and she'd always found that fact tempting and seductive and something she couldn't resist. She found herself sinking into him, responding to the desire she tasted in his kiss. She took his tongue into her mouth and let him explore, let him teach her again what passion was all about.

Passion. Chemistry. Sex. That had never been their problem.

Trust was.

Breaking away, she took a few steps back, wrapped her arms around herself and caught her breath. She could not trust Riley to put her best interests or Derek's first. Deep down, she still believed…

"What are you thinking?" he asked, his voice gruff as if the kiss had shaken him up, too.

"We can't let that happen. We can't! I have to keep Derek in mind. He could unite our families, or he could be a pawn between them."

"Do you think I'd use him?"

"I don't know," she said honestly.

For a moment he looked as if he were going to erupt. But then he shook his head, took a walk across the kitchen and then back to her again. "*You're* the one who left, Brenna. *You're* the one who walked away when I wanted to go public and tell everybody you were my girlfriend. So why won't you trust me?"

"Because I'll never know if you started an affair with me in high school because you really wanted me, or because you wanted to get back at my father."

Riley went completely still, and she could see defensive pride sliding over him once more. "If we're going to be Derek's parents, if we're going to make decisions about him together and decide what's best for his life, we have to figure out a way to trust each other."

"That could take some time," she pointed out.

The tension in the kitchen was thick enough to grab

and break in two. The snap and crackle of their attraction was like a force field surrounding them. She'd always felt drawn to Riley and now was no exception. But she knew she couldn't give in to that need to be held. She couldn't give in to the desire to let him kiss her. Not if she wanted to keep a clear head. Not if she wanted to make the right decisions for her and her son.

"I have to think of Derek first."

He must have seen that she meant it. He must have seen that everything was about their baby.

Rubbing his hand over his face, he decided, "We're going to pick out everything Derek needs together." Then he opened the refrigerator again, pulled out cheese and a quart of milk. "Let's eat lunch. We're both going to have to keep our strength up for whatever happens next."

Did he mean possibly running into her father? Or did he mean living under the same roof with *her?*

Brenna sat in Riley's guest bedroom and checked the alarm clock. It was after midnight and it wasn't Derek's soft baby sounds that were keeping her awake. She loved hearing those. She loved putting her hand on his little heart, making sure it was beating. No, what was keeping her awake was the way the whole afternoon had played out. Riley really didn't trust her any more than she trusted him. When he'd made that appointment with the pediatrician for tomorrow, she had to ask herself—did he really think she'd slept around? Did he really think she'd gone home to New York after the reunion and slept with someone else?

He was already acting like a dad, so maybe he *did* believe Derek was his. After they'd gotten home with all the supplies, and Derek had been fussy because he was overtired, Riley had taken him into his arms, rocked him, walked him, talked to him like a dad would. Every time he did, her heart broke a little bit because she'd be going back to New York and he'd be staying here. They hadn't talked about that in detail yet. That would be a humdinger of a conversation. It would be a few weeks until the DNA results came back, so maybe they'd put off the discussion until then.

With the windows open Brenna heard night sounds she'd forgotten. She was used to lights and sirens blaring, and horns honking and trucks rumbling even at night. She wasn't used to the silence any more, the call of the owls, the rustling of branches, the sometimes utter stillness. Scents of sage and pine drifted in the window as she heard Riley moving about in his room, heard the creak of his bed, the sound of the light switching on and off. Was he as restless as she was?

Maybe a bowl of cereal would help. That is, if Riley had cereal. She could always just have a glass of milk. The small crib on wheels they'd bought was set up beside the bed now. A mobile dangled on one side. She stood by it, looking down at her sleeping son. He was practically her whole world. Overnight she'd gone from a self-absorbed career woman to a mom. Derek had changed everything about her life.

But the career woman in her still had a to-do list. She'd have to check in with her store manager tomorrow, then with her fabric supplier, not to mention her PR consultant.

Time to get that cereal, she decided, stopping the racing thoughts.

Rubbing her hand in a full circle over Derek's back, she finally left him and went to the kitchen.

After opening two of the upper cupboards, she found what she was looking for and she had to smile. This was the same kind of cereal Riley liked in high school—sweet and sticky. Old times were the best times? Maybe that was true for her and Riley.

She was pouring cereal into a bowl when he entered the kitchen. She looked up and her breath practically stopped. He was shirtless and the waist button of his jeans was unsnapped. She couldn't seem to pull her gaze from all that black hair running a route down his chest.

"Want some company?" he asked.

"Can't sleep, either?" she might as well just ask.

"My head's too full of everything that's going on, about Derek and things I should do for him."

"And about me being under your roof? My parents not liking that idea one little bit?"

When he approached her and stopped right beside her, she wished she'd stayed in her room. He was all man, all temptation, all Riley, and he was close enough to touch.

"Having you under my roof is keeping me awake, too. Add *that* to your list." Desire was in his eyes and she could feel an answering response to it in her belly. So he wouldn't see it, she turned away, went to the refrigerator and pulled out the milk.

"You're running, Brenna."

"I'm not running. I'm turning away from what shouldn't happen. I'm getting a midnight snack. Do you want one or not?" She knew she was being defensive and that she wasn't handling the attraction between them very well. But she had to put some kind of barrier between them or they wouldn't only tumble into bed, they'd tumble into heartache.

He caught her arm and she stopped moving. Gazing up into his so-blue eyes, she felt her resistance melting away, and that wasn't good.

"Exactly how long are you going to stay in Miners Bluff?"

So that's what was bothering him. "A month. I have to get back to be ready for my fall show."

He looked somewhat relieved as if he'd expected her to say she'd be leaving at the end of the week.

She asked a question that had been in her mind all afternoon. "When are you going to tell your dad and the rest of your family about Derek?"

"I have to figure out the best way to do it."

"Best way?"

"My father's sober now. He has been for the past five years. I don't want to do anything that's going to rock that boat."

"My father never meant to destroy your dad's life. You've got to know that."

He appeared to measure his words carefully as he said, "No, I don't know that. I know your father was a ruthless businessman. All he cared about was expanding his department store. When my dad couldn't pay rent to him, your father took advantage of that. He stepped right in, and kicked him out."

"It was a *business* decision!"

Now Riley's composure cracked a little as bitterness seeped out. "Maybe he should have looked behind the business of it. My dad was already sinking financially and that made sure he sank. Then my mom didn't stick around because she was tired of four kids pulling on her, tired of hardly making ends meet, tired of being with a man who couldn't get back on his feet. After she left, Jack Daniels became Dad's best friend. Sometimes, I swear, he didn't even know we were around. If I hadn't worked at the grocery store and gotten day-old bread and expired meat, I'm not sure what would have happened."

Brenna had never known that things were that bad for the O'Rourkes. Oh, yes, she'd known her father had pushed Liam O'Rourke out of the restaurant so he could expand his department store. But she'd never known the rest.

"Riley, I'm sorry. I never knew. Even in high school, you never said."

"Back then, I was afraid of your opinion. I was afraid of *anyone's* opinion. The O'Rourkes stood on their own. They made do. They got by. Now we're all on our feet, even Dad. I don't want to do anything that might make him pick up that bottle again."

Maybe so. But Riley was forgetting something. "We went to my father's department store together and stopped for gas. Tomorrow we're going to the pediatrician. You know Miners Bluff. If your dad doesn't hear it from *you,* he's going to hear it from someone else very soon."

Riley's gaze told her he'd already thought of that, and he was worried about it.

Brenna stepped back to the cupboard and took out another cereal bowl, but Riley shook his head.

"Never mind. I think I'm going to go outside on the porch for a bit. Enjoy your snack."

She wanted to tell him he needed a shirt. She wanted to tell him the temperature had dipped like it always did at night here. But she didn't get the chance to tell him anything because he left the kitchen and went out the front door.

Riley still didn't want her pity. He still had his pride. He'd rather be cold than sit in the kitchen with her.

That thought tightened her throat.

Chapter Three

On Saturday morning Derek suckled as Brenna sat in the wooden rocker in her room. She rocked back and forth before the sun was up, wondering if there was any new mother in the world who wasn't sleep deprived. Not that she minded. She knew these moments with her child in her arms were precious because he was already growing fast. After all, she'd read all the baby books. Before long he'd be rolling over, sitting up, standing, crawling. She didn't want to think about all of that. She just wanted to enjoy Derek in her arms.

However, rocking couldn't prevent her from thinking about yesterday and the appointment with the pediatrician. She'd held Derek while the doctor swabbed the inside of his cheek and hers. Then she'd left the room with her son, knowing Riley was having his cheek swabbed, too.

She hoped just having the DNA test done would convince Riley he could trust her. Whenever they were in the same room, they didn't seem to know how to act!

After the appointment she'd taken Derek to visit with her mom for a few hours but her father had been at the store. She wanted to find her way somehow to a new father-daughter relationship better than the one she'd had since she'd left home.

Sounds suddenly broke the early morning quiet. Riley was up and about. Why? It was only 5:00 a.m. She heard the shower running and did her best not to imagine him under it. Then she heard drawers opening and closing. She'd been hoping to catch a few more hours of sleep. Instead, however, after she burped Derek and laid him back in his crib, she belted a robe tightly around her, opened her door wider and stepped out into the hall where shadows were thick and dark.

When Riley's door opened, he emerged, startling her. He took one look at her in her robe and frowned. "Problem?"

"No problem," she was quick to assure him. "I was feeding Derek and I heard you. What are you doing up?"

"Clay's coming by to pick up some gear. He's taking over my tour this morning so I can stay with you."

"There's no need for you to do that. I'm fine here with Derek on my own."

Riley took a step closer to her, maybe to see her better in the dim light that was glowing from his room into the hall. "This house is in the middle of nowhere. That's fine for me. But for you and the baby, I'm not so sure. I was supposed to take a group on a trail ride this morning and a tour out to Feather Peak tomorrow. If I do that, I'll be out of cell phone contact."

"You can't hover, Riley." She gave him a dark look and he knew exactly what that meant. Her parents had hovered all her life and she hadn't liked it one bit. It was one of the reasons she'd left.

His frown turned into a scowl. He looked as sexy as ever, dressed in a T-shirt and jeans, all muscles and fitness and virility. So much for *not* thinking about the night they'd spent together. It would be so easy to fall for him all over again, and she couldn't let that happen. She didn't want her heart broken. She knew exactly how Riley felt about marriage and couldn't forget the heartbreak from when she'd left before.

He was looking at her as if he'd like to unbelt her robe. He was looking at her with protective instincts that made her feel safe, yet seemed to threaten her at the same time. She didn't want to think about him as safe because nothing about Riley O'Rourke was secure.

Her independence was a cloak she wore easily and she wrapped it around herself now and stood up to him. "I'm a capable woman, Riley. I know I have a new baby, and who knows what can happen? But my parents are only a short drive away if I need anybody. You can't stop your life because of me and Derek. I wouldn't want you to."

Eyeing her warily, maybe not sure she meant what she was saying, he took another step closer. Riley within kissing or touching distance was not a good thing. But she didn't back away.

"Did you get much sleep?" he asked, suddenly changing the subject.

"Some," she answered cautiously.

"You know, if you'd let me give Derek a bottle you could get more sleep."

"And you'd get less."

"Fifty-fifty. Isn't that what parenting is about?"

She wasn't sure how to answer that one. Yes, she

wanted her son to know his father. But they had different lives, lived in different places, and she didn't know how they were going to settle that.

"I'll start using a bottle with Derek some of the time. If you want to feed him, you can."

"I'd like that." His voice had gone all low and husky and she heard the emotion in it, something Riley usually hid. Was it the idea of taking care of his son? Experiences he'd had that had shown him how precious life could be?

As quickly as he'd taken a step toward her, he took a step back.

"All right," he said, going back to their earlier conversation. "I'll call Clay and tell him I'm taking out the tours. But today I'll be back by 1:00. I need to call my family and let the fallout begin."

She'd watched him pace at times yesterday, pick up his phone and then put it down. He had a lot more family than she did, so there would be many more judgments to combat. No wonder he'd waited until he knew what he wanted to say…and do.

"I'll be here," she said softly. "While Derek sleeps, I need to work."

"Work as in—"

"New sketches, new designs, phone calls. I have good people working for me, but they still need to consult with me."

He nodded as if he understood. Then as if he couldn't help himself, he reached out and touched her cheek. "Go back to bed. You have blue smudges under your eyes."

Abruptly he turned away and headed for the kitchen.

As Brenna returned to her room, she knew she was probably going to have blue smudges for the next few months. Who did Riley see when he looked at her? The girl he'd known? Or the woman she'd become?

It really didn't matter...because nothing had changed between them. On the other hand, *everything* had.

Riley was supposed to meet the tourists he'd be leading on a trail ride at the Rocky D ranch. Zack Decker guided a few horses into the corral to choose from—a pretty gray-spotted appaloosa, a bay, a chestnut, and Riley's favorite, Silver Star, a beautiful pewter-gray gelding who was as reliable as he was durable. He was Riley's pick every time.

Zack grinned at him as Riley strode up to the horse and gave him his hand to smell.

Silver whinnied a greeting.

Riley gave him a "hey, boy," and stroked his neck.

"What's on for this morning?" Zack asked.

"Three businessmen who decided to take a vacation together and come West."

"Do you think they know how to ride?" Zack asked with wry sarcasm.

"They say they've had some experience. But trail riding in the foothills of Moonshadow Mountain is a heck of a lot different than riding on groomed lanes outside a big city. So we'll see."

"Do you think you'll be able to ride out and be back by lunch?"

"It'll be tight, but we should do okay. I really don't want it to go long."

As Zack walked around Silver and checked the lead on another horse's nose, he said, "You usually don't care if the trail ride goes all day."

"The men are driving to Flagstaff and have a meeting about hiking down the Grand Canyon."

"What's the *but*?" Zack asked bluntly.

Zack never beat around the bush. As a movie producer and director as well as co-manager of the Rocky D with his wife Jenny, he could put his thumb right on the pertinent point even when you didn't want him to. Riley knew Brenna's presence in town wouldn't be quiet forever. He was going to put in that call to his father when he got back and meet with him later today.

But for the meantime there would be no harm in telling Zack because he'd become more than a former classmate—he'd become a loyal friend.

"I had a surprise the other day."

"Good surprise or bad surprise?" Zack asked, propping a foot on the bottom rung of the fence, tilting his Stetson back with his other hand.

"Brenna McDougall returned to Miners Bluff and ended up on my doorstep."

"I heard you were talking at the reunion and left together. Family feud over?"

"Hell, no. But…I didn't tell you why she came back."

"If she was on your doorstep, then it was to see you."

"Did you take a class in deductive theory?"

"Get on with it, O'Rourke. You want to tell me something. You know you do. You're just having trouble doing it."

Riley sighed, gazed off into the distance where pines and aspen, larch and laurel gave the Rocky D its special charm. "Have you ever done anything foolish, Zack? So foolish it changed the rest of your life?"

"Not speaking to my father for all those years was foolish. Not convincing Jenny to go with me out of high school was foolish. Holding grudges for too long without knowing the real reason behind them was foolish. So, yeah, I've done foolish things." Zack had reconciled with his father Silas and had married Jenny less than a year ago. He sure seemed happy.

But Riley didn't believe in marriage. He'd been too hurt by his parents. He didn't believe two people could make promises that would last forever. His mother couldn't stand the heat and she'd gotten out of the kitchen. His mother's abandonment of her family had driven his dad to the bottle. Liam O'Rourke had never gotten over loving his wife and not being loved in return. Those difficult years had had a profound effect on Riley.

And if Brenna hadn't been able to stand by Riley during the tough times, had *she* ever really loved *him?*

He had to admit when he saw Zack and Jenny together, they looked at each other as if they were each other's worlds. He realized the same was true for Clay Sullivan and his wife, Celeste, who had also reunited after the reunion, as well as Mikala Conti and Dawson Barrett who had been classmates and were now expecting a baby. But besides his own parents' divorce and that of his brother Patrick, he'd seen his sister lose a husband she'd loved.

The bottom-line truth was all of that plus Riley's tours of service had affected him deeply. He didn't want to be tied down. He wanted room to roam and that prevented romantic entanglements from going any further. Still…

Whenever he thought of Derek, he thought about a life built around his son. He just couldn't envision it yet.

"Brenna knocked on my door and when I opened it she was holding my baby," he blurted out.

Zack didn't react at first. Then he asked with that perception Riley didn't know if he admired or hated, "This happened the night of the reunion?"

"Yeah."

"What are you going to do about it?"

"I'm a dad. I'm going to *act* like a dad."

"She has her picture in magazines, doesn't she? Jenna told me she's a well-known bridal gown designer. Mikala wore one of her gowns for her wedding."

"Seriously?"

"Dawson told her whatever she wanted and that's what she wanted. Small wedding, really nice gown. Not that I noticed much, with Jenny in a dress Brenna designed, too."

"Yeah, she's famous—in New York, anyway, maybe in L.A. We haven't gotten into it."

"Well, you'd better. I imagine her life is as busy as life could get." Zack shook his head. "How did you ever get involved with her again? Your families will never see eye-to-eye."

"Not even over a grandson?"

After a moment of letting that question sit, Zack asked, "So, what's his name?"

"His name's Derek."

"Don't think Derek is going to solve all your problems. Especially not the ones between you and Brenna."

"How do you know we *have* problems?"

"You hooked up the night of the reunion. She went back to New York and you were here. Did you have contact with her afterward?"

"No," Riley said tersely.

"Like I said, problems. What are you going to do?"

"Let it play out a little. Then I have to decide if I'm ready to make any changes. Derek is important to me, Zack. More important than anything ever has been."

"Then you'll figure it out."

The sound of a Suburban's engine signaled the arrival of Riley's businessmen. This morning he was going to try to forget about Brenna and Derek. He was going to focus on the trail and his clients and appreciating everything this beautiful country had to offer.

Riley turned into the lane leading to his house. A quarter of a mile and a curve later he saw the truck parked in his driveway and he stomped on the accelerator, leaving a rooster tail of gravel behind him. His father's truck. His dad was in his house with Brenna and the baby. He could only imagine what might be going on in there.

Leaving his trail gear exactly where it was, not even grabbing his hat, he climbed out of the vehicle, slammed the door and rushed up the front walk. After he pushed open the door and stepped inside…he froze.

Brenna was hovering by the sofa, looking worried. His father was sitting on the couch, holding Derek carefully in the crook of his arm. He'd been running his finger over his grandson's chin when Riley opened the door.

Now he stopped and turned toward his son. "Just when were you going to tell me about this?" he demanded.

Riley hated the fact that this had happened to Brenna, that she'd had to deal with his dad all on her own. He just wished he knew what she'd said and how she'd explained it all. He just wished he'd picked up the phone yesterday.

Brenna looked upset, maybe a little tense, but not angry. Another woman in this spot might have been furious this had happened to her.

Score another point for Brenna.

"Brenna just arrived a few days ago," Riley said,

knowing that was a lame explanation. He felt grimy, as if he'd ridden through a dust bowl—and he practically had.

His father shifted Derek a little, still looking down at him. Then he turned his attention to Riley again. "Brenna told me the two of you told *her* parents and then you went to the doc to get a DNA test yesterday."

Riley's gaze shot to hers.

She gave a little shrug.

"You don't think you're the dad?" Liam asked, now staring straight at him.

Riley stroked his hand down over his face. "This is private business between me and Brenna."

His father studied him. "Maybe. Maybe not. Tell me when you were planning to notify me I had a grandson."

"Today, Pop. I was going to call you when I got back from a trail ride this morning."

Liam looked at Riley for a long moment and then nodded. "You don't lie. I know that. I just feel a little… out of the loop. Do your brothers and sister know?"

"They will now," Riley muttered.

"Mr. O'Rourke, can I get you something to drink?" Brenna asked. "I have iced tea, soda—"

Again Liam looked at Riley, giving him a half smile, as if to say, *She's acting as mistress of the house*. Riley was a little surprised at that, too, but maybe she just wanted to escape the room. Maybe she *was* really angry but not showing it. *Maybe* a lot of things.

"Do you have any coffee?" Liam asked. "I'm working the supper shift and will be at the restaurant till late. Some caffeine roaring through my veins would be great."

"Is the coffee in the canister, Riley?" Brenna asked.

"You don't drink coffee?" Liam asked.

"Not while I'm breastfeeding."

Liam had black hair shot with silver, blue eyes and a ruddy complexion that just grew ruddier. "I see. Never thought of that. I admire women who put their baby's welfare first."

Riley and Brenna both knew exactly why that was. Shawna O'Rourke hadn't had the fortitude, or the compassion, or the love a mother should have for her children, to stay.

His father shifted toward Brenna now. "So, what did your parents have to say? I'll bet your dad popped a blood vessel."

To Riley's relief, Brenna retained her composure. "I've been living in New York ever since I left after high school, so I'm on my own. I make my own decisions, Mr. O'Rourke. Now I don't depend on my parents for anything. Not even their opinion of what I should or shouldn't do."

"But you did once."

"Yes, I did."

"I knew you and Riley were an item, even if *they* didn't. But Riley wanted to keep it a secret, so I pretended I didn't know. My gut tells me Miners Bluff was just a little too small for you."

"I wanted a career Miners Bluff couldn't give me."

"And you got it. Do you think your life's a lot different than it would have been if you'd stayed?"

"Pop! *Stop* with the questions," Riley erupted.

"I'm just trying to figure out what's happening now. How are you going to be a father to your son when he's in New York and you're here?"

That was the question they were all asking.

"I'll get that coffee." Brenna didn't move right away. Rather, she went to Derek first to make sure he was safe in Liam's arms.

"I held four kids at one time or another," he assured her. "I never dropped one of them. And I'm sober. Have been for five years."

"I didn't mean to suggest anything otherwise. He's just so small. Even when Riley holds him, I feel I want to put a safety net underneath him."

His dad chuckled at that and really looked at Brenna. "We didn't get to know each other when you were in high school."

"No, sir. We didn't."

"You really are an honest woman, aren't you?"

"I hope so. I picked up a box of cookies that aren't home-baked, but they're good. Be right back."

Riley couldn't look away from her for a couple of moments. She'd tied her hair back in a ponytail. She was wearing jeans and a beaded T-shirt. Her belted waist showed her slimness. Her legs were long and curvy. Her feet were bare.

While his father played with Derek's fingers and toes, Riley followed Brenna to the kitchen. At the doorway, he lowered his voice. "I never expected this to happen."

"When your dad first arrived, he was throwing questions at me. He was really upset, Riley."

Riley studied her face, so temptingly pretty. "And what about you?"

She looked up at him, her gaze hiding nothing. "I'm okay."

Riley sighed. "Best laid plans. I shouldn't have waited. So why didn't you just make small talk until I got here? Geez, Brenna, telling him about the DNA test."

"Do you *know* your father?"

There was a note in her tone that warned him to be cautious. "I probably know him better than anyone. Why?"

She practically whispered, "Your father asked me detailed questions. What time I got in on Wednesday. What we did that night, then yesterday. 'Oh, you went to the doctor's. Just to get him checked?' Was I supposed to lie? He would have seen it. He's a great lie detector. I can tell."

Riley almost smiled at that. "We all used to think that, before he started the heavy drinking. Now that he's not drinking again, I guess you could say he's more perceptive."

"Yes, well, he guessed it wasn't just a regular doctor's appointment, so I had to tell him the truth."

"You're an open book," Riley said, meaning it as a compliment.

But she shook her head. "No, I'm not. Not anymore."

"You got hurt?"

"Oh, I got hurt."

The idea of Brenna hurt disturbed something deep in Riley. He dropped his arm around her shoulder and guided her deeper into the kitchen. "Come on, let's give him a little alone time with his grandson. I doubt if he's going to get much of that. As soon as Shannon knows, she'll be here wanting to hold him, too."

"And how about your brothers?"

Riley's expression must have hinted at trouble there.

"Tell me."

"There's nothing to tell. I don't know how they'll feel."

"But you have an inkling."

"We're the O'Rourkes. You're the McDougalls. My brothers consider our two families to have a feud going on. So I don't know what will happen when they hear."

After Riley found the coffee, Brenna quickly made a pot. As the coffee brewed, the two of them just stared at each other, wondering what came next. When Brenna finally asked if he had a tray, he looked at her as if she were crazy.

"A tray, Riley, to carry in his mug and some sugar and creamer. Surely there's something like that somewhere."

They looked and looked until she found a flat platter that would suffice. When she carried it out to Liam and set it on the coffee table, he looked at it as if it were foreign. "Just the mug would have been fine."

"Do you take cream or sugar?"

"Just a spot of cream."

She'd laid a spoon on the tray, too. "Would you like me to take Derek now?"

"I get it. You don't trust me holding him with a cup of coffee in my other hand."

"I think he needs to be changed and then maybe a little nap. He gets cranky when he doesn't get enough sleep. Sort of like your son."

Liam practically roared at that, his first real laugh. "So you know that about him, do you?"

"I haven't been around him for a while, but I do remember that. You're welcome to stay as long as you'd like. I can wheel his crib in here if you'd like to watch him sleep."

"You're serious, aren't you?" Liam asked.

"Sure. Babies sleep so much of the time at this age. If you want to capture their expressions and just be around them, it's easier that way."

"You've been around babies a lot?"

"Oh, no. But I have read a lot of articles, blogs and books. They all help."

"Is there anything in your books about a situation like this, where one side of the family thinks the other side of the family sucks?"

"All right, Dad. We're not going to get into it. I don't want you all riled up."

"You think I'll pick up a bottle again?"

Riley's silence spoke volumes.

His father sighed. "We're going to have to get into it, boy. It's the only way we'll get over it. I don't want to see Angus McDougall any more than you do. But I have a feeling we're going to run into each other *now*."

Derek had become more unsettled and was now squirming a bit. Brenna could apparently see that Riley's dad looked uncomfortable with a fussy baby.

Crossing to him she held out her hands for her son and his dad helped her gather the baby close. Then she said, "I'll change him."

His dad rose. "I have to be going. I have computer work to do at the restaurant before our midafternoon crowd turns into the supper crowd. I suppose I'll be seeing more of you, Brenna, and I hope more of Derek. Unless you'd rather keep him away from me?"

Already headed for the hall, she stopped and turned. "I see no need to keep him away from you. You can visit anytime you want." Then she hurried down the hall.

Liam stuffed his hands in his jeans pockets. "Do you think she meant that?"

"From what I've seen so far of her, she doesn't say what she doesn't mean."

His father started toward the door and Riley followed. Liam stopped, eyed his son and asked, "So, are you the dad or not? Do you want to tell me what happened?"

How much to say, and how much to keep private? "The night of the reunion Brenna and I danced and actually began talking. I asked her back here to catch up."

"Oh, the two of you caught up, all right. That's easy to see."

"What do you mean it's easy to see?"

"Other than Derek, you mean?"

"Yes, other than Derek."

"You look at her as if you want her."

Geez. His dad could see that?

"I remember the way you two were in high school. You thought I was drunk. I wasn't always. I saw you sneak into the back of your car. I saw you sneak into the old shed at the back of the property. And I knew what was going on."

What could Riley say to that?

"So why the DNA test? You putting her through hoops?" his father asked.

"I didn't know who Brenna had become since she'd gone away. It's been fifteen years, Dad. She turns up here on my doorstep, says Derek's my baby, and I'm just supposed to believe that?"

"If you trust her word, you do. But I know you don't trust women. And I know why. So if you need the DNA test, then you need one. But I do want to know why you didn't call me the night she arrived."

This was one of the hardest questions Riley would have to answer. "I didn't call because I felt I had enough on my hands dealing with her and Derek."

After a long, narrow look, his dad nodded. "I'll accept that. But from now on if something happens here with Brenna or Derek or you, I want to be called first. I've been behind Angus McDougall all my life. It's not going to happen now. Not when my grandson's involved."

Riley understood exactly how his father felt. He clasped his dad's shoulder. "It won't happen again. You have my word."

Whatever Brenna did, whatever Angus McDougall

did, Riley would not let the McDougalls come between him and his father. He finally had a relationship with his dad and that wasn't going to get messed up because he'd been too stupid to use a condom. Brenna would have to come to terms with the fact that her family didn't come first, not with him.

Chapter Four

After Liam left, Brenna rinsed the coffee carafe.

Riley stood by the refrigerator and thought she was being entirely too quiet. "I'm going to have to make a grocery store run. If you write a list, I can pick up whatever you want."

She stopped rinsing. "We could all go."

"Already going stir-crazy?" He was half serious and half joking. With the life she was leading in New York, she'd never be happy back here, stuck in the middle of nowhere.

"It would be good to get out. When I'm here, I think too much."

He went over to the sink where she was standing. "Thinking about what?"

"You, and me and Derek, and what's going to happen next."

Standing here so close to her, he knew what *he*

wanted to happen next. She seemed to read his mind. He could have sworn the pulse at her throat sped up.

She said, "The history between us could get in the way of making good decisions."

"You don't mean history, you mean chemistry. Just say it like it is, Brenna."

Her face flushed. "It's worse than an elephant in the room," she murmured. "I can't—"

Once Brenna got started, her thought process could make him dizzy, and he only knew one way to stop it. He slid his hand under her hair, pulled her toward him and kissed her. Her breath sighed into his, right before desire took over and neither of them thought about breathing. Her body had always fit against his so perfectly. Her mouth had always been sweet, soft and more potent than any liquor he'd ever tasted. Brenna's passion had always matched his.

This afternoon it came alive, as it had the night of the reunion, arousing him, pushing him to remember, making him wish they'd had no history to interfere. As she moaned and his hand went to her breast, he buried caution and good sense in favor of taking what she offered.

...Until her cell phone on the counter played the wedding march!

It only took a few seconds for that sound to clear his head. And by that time Brenna was pushing away, looking as if she'd committed a major sin, snatching her phone from the counter.

Pretending the kiss hadn't shaken him up, he arched a brow at the music.

"My store manager," she explained, taking the call and walking into the living room, glancing over her shoulder, then concentrating on the conversation.

Riley decided to load the dishwasher with the dishes in the sink, but listened to every word Brenna said.

"It's okay, Michelle. I understand. You don't want to lose a client. *We* don't want to lose a client. But I'm not returning to New York…for a while. I'm not sure of the exact date."

"I understand she wants a one-of-a-kind gown. So we can do a couple of things. She can phone conference with me. She can videoconference with me. From what she tells me, I'll draw up three sketches and then we can go from there."

"No, I can't fly back, even overnight. I'm not going to put Derek through that and I don't want to leave him. If we lose her, we lose her."

Riley slid a dish into place. Brenna had come to Miners Bluff for a reason—to introduce him to his son. It seemed she'd do everything in her power to have nothing interfere with that.

Yet how long could she ignore business? Just how long would she be satisfied with staying here among pines, deer and elk?

He listened less intently as she talked to her store manager about day-to-day operations—a seamstress getting sick, material being flown in, models they were choosing for the fall show. By the time Brenna ended her call Riley realized she *was* running a business, a business grounded in New York. She had a full life there, just as he had one here. He'd missed his family and he liked them coming around. He liked the peace he'd found. But if his son was in New York City—

Maybe joint custody would work. Would Brenna consider it? As she entered the kitchen again he knew *now* was not the time to discuss it. Especially not with the fire from that kiss still leaving smoke in its wake.

"Maybe you should go to the grocery store alone," she said.

"Because of the kiss? Or because of your phone call?" He wasn't going to let that kiss throw her into a tailspin. That's why he'd kissed her to begin with, to keep her tailspin from whirling out of control.

"I have to go over supply orders and I'm expecting a call back from a client...an important client."

"*Important* meaning she's rich?"

"*Important* meaning I designed a dress for one of her daughters and she and her daughter loved it. She has two more daughters. I don't just sell gowns, Riley, I sell a unique service that's based on relationships."

He felt petty for suggesting she was only interested in the money. But that kiss had gotten to him, too. It sure *was* an elephant in the room. "I didn't mean to suggest—"

"Yes, you did. You've always had a problem with my family being well-off. I have to admit I live a good life, but not an extravagant one. And I work hard to make my business thrive. So don't suggest I'm all about money, because I'm not. I never have been."

That one hit home. She never would have dated him, snuck around with him if a guy her parents approved of had been on her mind. Suddenly he wanted to know, "If my name hadn't been O'Rourke, would you have stayed in Miners Bluff?"

"You mean if our families hadn't been at war but you'd come from a working class family? Would that have made a difference?"

"Exactly."

"It might have. Our families being at war was just too big an obstacle to overcome. We should have known that from the beginning."

"We were kids with raging hormones. We didn't think rationally."

When Brenna tilted her head and studied him as if she was trying to see clear through him, he felt a guilty pang. Dating Brenna might have started out as revenge, a way to hurt her dad. But it had ended much differently. She still seemed to be trying to figure it out.

"The night of the reunion we weren't kids," she reminded him.

"No, we were adults who should have known better. But we can't kick ourselves into next year for being human, for being in the right place with the wrong person." As soon as those words came out of his mouth he knew he'd stuck his foot in it.

"Wrong person? Who would you rather have been with?"

"I didn't mean it like that, Brenna. I didn't have somebody specific in mind. I just meant—"

"You just meant that we were never right for each other because there were so many reasons why we were wrong." Spinning away from him, she went to the refrigerator and took down the notepad that hung there by a magnet. Then she snatched a pen from the counter. "I'm going to check on Derek and then make a list of what we need."

A list. So he could go to the grocery store—alone. If the three of them had gone they'd look like a family. But they wouldn't *be* a family.

Late that afternoon, Riley carried in grocery bags, handling two at a time in each hand. Brenna watched the play of muscles under his T-shirt as he settled them on the kitchen table. She herself was carrying Derek in one of those slings that rested on her chest. He was asleep after a fussy spell. She'd wheeled his crib into the living room while she'd worked on the sofa, but that hadn't lasted long. Now she slipped him from the sling and laid him in the crib again. This time he didn't awaken.

When she returned to the kitchen, Riley was stowing the groceries into the cupboards and the refrigerator. She couldn't seem to pull her eyes away from him.

"Did you get much work done?" he asked, as he bent over to push something onto the shelf in the refrigerator.

He had great buns. He had great everything.

He glanced over his shoulder. "Brenna?"

Concentrating, she remembered the question he'd asked. "Some. Derek didn't want to settle down after he ate so I walked him for a while. Did you know the lilacs along the side of the house are blooming?"

With a sly grin, he asked, "You remember how flowers grow?"

She poked him in the arm. "New York isn't all sidewalks and tall buildings." Taking a box of cereal from a bag, she pushed it in the top cupboard.

He said, "I put away the perishables. Leave that for now. Come into the living room. I want to show you something."

"Something you bought?"

"Yeah, something I bought."

She wandered into the living room and peeked at Derek while Riley went outside. It wasn't long before he returned, carrying a new bag. Inside there was a foot-and-a-half-tall box. He motioned for her to sit on the sofa. After she did, he sat beside her, took the box from the bag and set it on her lap.

She could see a plush, tan bear through the plastic.

"It's not just a stuffed toy. It has a computer chip inside. When you press its tummy, it turns on a sound like a mom's womb. It's supposed to help babies sleep."

She just stared at the box, warm feelings for Riley percolating up all over the place.

"Come on. Open it."

When she lifted the flap and removed the bear, she saw it was soft and fluffy, the kind of toy any child would want.

Riley pressed the bear's tummy and a soft whooshing started. It sounded like the sloshing of water.

"I'll have to try this if he won't go back to sleep tonight. Thank you." She pressed the stomach to stop the sound. "It was thoughtful of you to buy this."

"I saw it the other day when we were shopping for supplies. Then I wasn't sure. Today I was."

"Did his crying keep you awake last night?"

"Not any more than it kept you awake. Why didn't you come get me?"

She could skirt the issue, or she could tell him the truth. "In the middle of the night like that, when he's crying and I'm in my nightgown, I feel vulnerable. It isn't the best time to go toe-to-toe with you."

"Toe-to-toe or lips-to-lips?" His voice was almost challenging in a seductive way. Their gazes connected and held as she squeezed the bear under her fingers to keep from touching Riley. But he seemed to have their lips on his mind because he leaned closer. She swayed toward him, but thoughts flew through her head in the briefest of seconds. Was he trying to get on her good side with the gift? Did he think kissing her would persuade her to stay?

Suddenly there was a knock on the door. Riley leaned back and Brenna sat up straight.

"Hello," a feminine voice called. "Anybody home?"

Derek started crying.

Riley swore.

Brenna was glad for the interruption. As soon as the woman stepped inside, Brenna recognized her. It was Shannon, Riley's younger sister. Her hair was auburn, but she had Riley's blue eyes.

"You woke him," Riley accused her.

"Babies wake up and they fall asleep again. That's what they do."

Setting the bear on the sofa, Brenna stood and greeted Shannon, not knowing what Riley's sister was going to think of her being here. "Hi."

Shannon looked Brenna over in that way one woman has of assessing another. Brenna did the same to her. And then they smiled at each other.

"Do you have children?" Brenna asked.

"A little boy. Jakie's four."

Riley said, "And a great kid. Shannon's raising him on her own. Her husband was a bull rider and he got killed the year after Jakie was born."

"Oh, I'm so sorry," Brenna said, meaning it. "So you know what it's like to be a single mom."

"Indeed I do. I have something for you," she told her brother.

"What?"

"Be right back." She must have put the present on the porch before she'd come in, because she leaned out the door, got a hold of something and pulled it inside. It was a stroller. A very nice stroller. Brenna had been thinking of buying one herself and leaving it here. Her friends in New York had given her one at her shower. But she would have liked one today when Derek was restless.

Brenna went over to it immediately. "Oh, it's terrific. It has a canopy and everything."

"And the little toys on the tray to keep him occupied when he's older," Shannon explained. "It's from the whole family."

Brenna looked up just in time to see some kind of silent communication pass between brother and sister. She didn't understand what it was about.

"Will Sean and Patrick be stopping in sometime?" Brenna asked. She hadn't seen Riley's brothers since she'd left Miners Bluff. One was older than Riley, the other younger.

"They say they'll stop in another time. They didn't want to intrude and overwhelm you with O'Rourkes."

But Brenna caught Riley's scowl. Something more was going on than his brothers not wanting to intrude.

"Is my presence here keeping them from coming to see their nephew?"

Riley shook his head at his sister, but she didn't seem to heed his warning. "Sean and Patrick are locked in the past like my father is sometimes. But the truth is, if Dad holds Derek often enough, I think he'll put the past where it belongs."

"And where do you think that is?" Riley asked his sister.

"How long ago did Angus McDougall *steal* Pop's restaurant?" Shannon asked.

Brenna felt a flare of anger, but then she realized Shannon was just repeating in a mocking way the story she'd heard so many times.

Riley glanced at Brenna as if to gauge her reaction. "Shannon."

"Seriously, Riley, how long ago?" his sister asked again.

"About twenty-five years."

"So, isn't that long enough to put it all to rest?"

"It's not that simple."

"Well, it should be. We've all gotten past it. Dad's sober now and has his life together. You're a decorated veteran. Patrick has a bike shop and Sean's accounting firm has taken off. We're all fine."

"Grudges are hard to erase," Brenna said, wishing it weren't so, wishing she could trust Riley, whether it came to dealings about their son or about their personal relationship.

"Does *your* father still hold a grudge against *my* dad?" Shannon asked.

Brenna considered tidbits she'd heard from her dad over the years. "I haven't talked to him about it in a long time. I know there are still business owners in the community who won't deal with my father because of the reputation they feel he has. That reputation came largely from what your father said about him."

She held up her hand to stop comments from both Shannon and Riley. "The truth is—I'm tired of the whole thing, too. But I'm afraid my return and bringing Derek here has stirred hard feelings up."

Shannon shook her head. She walked over to the crib and gazed down at her nephew. "He's beautiful. He could pull our families together again, instead of tearing them apart. We should see if we can make that happen," she said to Riley.

"We can't force anything."

Brenna was wondering if he was thinking about his own feelings.

"No, not force them. But we can gently consider alternatives." She turned to Brenna. "If you ever need a babysitter, just let me know. Jakie's a good little boy. I know he'd like having a baby around."

"Where is he now?" Brenna asked.

"He's at a friend's house for an after-school playdate." She checked her watch. "I have to pick him up."

"Thank you again for the stroller, and for your willingness to try to bridge the gap between our families."

Shannon glanced at Riley. "I think women are better at that than men." Then before her brother could make a comment, she smiled and left the house.

Brenna's throat felt thick with emotion as she cleared it. "I never knew your sister very well."

"She was four years younger than we were, just a kid back then."

"A wise woman now."

"My brothers and sister and I might squabble, but we stick together. They'll all come around. They have to because Derek is part of their family now."

But Brenna was very aware Derek was a McDougall, not an O'Rourke. Whether his brothers accepted Derek or not was a huge thing for her.

"Hey," Riley said. "What are you thinking about?"

Could he still read her so easily? Or was she just that transparent right now, unable to guard herself completely or hide her emotions behind neutrality like he did? Only he didn't look neutral now.

He looked as if he understood. "We'll make a family, Brenna, one way or another."

She wasn't sure what he meant by that. When Derek was with him, he'd a have a family here—uncles and aunts and cousins and a grandfather. And when Derek was with Brenna, he'd have his grandparents and her friends in New York. Couldn't that be just as good as what Riley could offer?

Except...Derek wouldn't have his dad.

She had the sudden urge to tell Riley something he

didn't know. "You haven't asked me about Derek's middle name."

Riley looked taken aback, as if he hadn't even thought of that. Or maybe he had because he said, "I thought you'd give him a strong, Scottish middle name after one of Angus's ancestors."

Was he trying to pick a fight? Was he trying to put distance between them? She couldn't seem to do that when Derek was the subject of their conversation. She didn't bristle. She didn't get defensive.

Rather, she took a step closer to him. "Derek's middle name is Ryan. Derek, a good Scottish name for my family, and Ryan, an Irish name for yours."

She saw a different look now come into Riley's eyes. Oh, there was surprise. But right behind it was that tenderness for her…for Derek. He took that all-important step toward her, wrapped his arms around her and pulled her close for a hug.

Resting his chin on top of her head, he said, "Maybe having Derek will fix things."

For a moment she thought about the possibility that he was right. But then she knew otherwise. Derek couldn't heal the past between them. The adults had to do it themselves. She didn't know if the O'Rourkes or the McDougalls could change points of view, could put themselves in each other's shoes, could let grudges melt away like winter snow.

The hug brought comfort for only a few seconds, then bodies against bodies created more than comfort. She couldn't be this close to Riley and not want to touch him, not want to scrape his shirt up his flat stomach and run her fingers through his chest hair. Not want to touch her thumb to his lips because they were so worthy of attention. He smelled musky and outdoorsy and altogether enticing.

Riley must have been finding their closeness a turn-on, too, because she felt him get aroused. The excitement of just standing there like that made it difficult to breathe. But she knew what she had to do for herself *and* Derek. Riley still had doubts that Derek was his son. She had doubts about what he'd felt for her in the first place, so many years ago. They had no business falling into this attraction again. This time if something happened with Riley, they'd complicate their lives too much to parent together. She wanted Riley in Derek's life for Derek's sake.

So she pulled away, mumbled an excuse about pumping breast milk, took Derek's crib and wheeled it back to the guest bedroom.

While Riley stood in the living room…alone.

Brenna worked late into the night while Derek slept. But even now the tension between her and Riley seemed to permeate the house. She wished she could do something to alleviate it, but she didn't know what. She had to keep up with the designs that were marking her place in the fashion world. The only way to do that was to work when all was quiet, when Derek slept. Maybe she'd catch up on sleep when he was three, she thought wryly.

She was finishing details on an almost perfect sketch when Derek began crying. Checking the clock, she saw it was after midnight.

"Well, little buddy," she said, lifting him out of his crib, "that was a long nap. Thank you very much. I got a lot done."

But thanks didn't seem to be what he wanted. He was

batting his fists in the air and his little face was turning red, as he did his version of shouting to be fed.

If there was a rap on the door, Brenna didn't hear it. But all at once Riley was there at the foot of the bed watching her jiggle Derek. "Need help?"

Riley had told her he'd be leaving before dawn to take his group of tourists on horseback to Feather Peak. However, he'd felt shut out of Derek's life so far and she knew he was thinking about when she returned to New York.

"I have breast milk in the refrigerator. If you'd like to feed him, I can warm it up."

"Are you all right with that? I mean, physically." His face turned a little ruddy and she had to smile.

Riley knew if Derek didn't nurse, she'd have to pump her breasts. That probably wasn't something he wanted to discuss. On the other hand it was considerate of him to ask. "I'll take care of it while you're feeding Derek. Don't you have a trip planned for the morning out to Feather Peak?"

"Yeah, I do."

They were practically shouting over Derek's crying. But she saw something in Riley's eyes that made her wonder just how peaceful his sleep usually was. Yes, the night of the reunion he'd fallen asleep after they'd made love. But maybe that usually didn't happen so easily. Maybe he'd come home from his service with insomnia like many veterans had. Many veterans came home with a lot worse. Riley had been very, very lucky.

But as he took Derek from her arms, she realized luck had only been a part of it. He'd probably been very skilled at what he did, and he'd always had the will to survive.

She thought, not for the first time, about the differences between Riley O'Rourke and Thad Johnson. Riley's service had essentially been selfless. Thad had been all about success and reaching his next financial goal. Riley had deep family values. Thad had been unfaithful and cavalier about it.

There really was no comparison.

"I hope it doesn't take long to warm up that milk," he said now.

"Not long at all."

He was holding Derek, trying to comfort him, but his eyes passed over her in her nightgown, a satin thing she used when she traveled because it didn't take up much room. Now, however, she realized it certainly didn't hide very much, either. He could see every curve and slope, and her nipples....

She grabbed for her robe at the foot of the bed, slipped it on and belted it, then hurried to the kitchen.

A few minutes later she was back, handing Riley the bottle, watching him as he positioned Derek in his arm then teased his son's lips with the nipple. Derek latched onto it hungrily and Riley chuckled. Brenna had always liked the sound of his laugh, the sound of his voice.

He spoke to his son in soft, comforting words. "You're getting to be such a big boy. Look at you drinking all that."

Brenna felt her heart melting all over again.

After a couple of ounces, Brenna said, "You have to burp him."

She took a clean hand towel that had been folded on the dresser and handed it to Riley. "Here, toss this over your shoulder. You never know what will happen with a baby."

She couldn't help looking at his shoulder as she said it, all that chest hair, his washboard abs. She stopped there. Either her hormones were still all stirred up or her attraction to Riley had gone over the top. Over the top, because her heart was racing, her breathing was becoming more shallow and she felt her skin heat because he was sitting there in nothing but sleeping shorts and she wasn't wearing all that much herself.

As Riley helped Derek to his shoulder and gently rubbed his son's back, Brenna couldn't stay in the room with him. She just couldn't. "Are you okay with him while I take care of things?"

"Sure," he said with one of those slow smiles that always curled her toes.

Chapter Five

When dawn broke Riley was already gone. Brenna hadn't even heard him leave. She must have fallen into a deep sleep after he'd laid Derek in his crib then bid her good-night. She thought that good-night had carried…something. The same something she saw in his eyes when she knew he wanted to kiss her. Staying here with him was awkward, yet it seemed only fair.

When she thought about a month of hearing Riley in his bedroom, of running into him in the kitchen, of watching him with Derek…

She took Derek for a walk, noticing the sun teetering behind the clouds. The scents of pine and peonies reacquainted her with some of the beauty of Miners Bluff. She even caught sight of a deer flashing across the rear of Riley's backyard. She wouldn't go far, not with Derek, but she appreciated the scents of summer coming on, the sight of dew on grass and bushes, the feel of the almost-mountain air on her cheeks. Had she missed Miners Bluff? Yes. Did she want to live here again? She couldn't. Not if she wanted to meet her responsibilities, to raise Derek the way she wanted to raise him.

Without a father? a little voice asked.

She didn't have the answer.

Riley had left a note saying he'd be back midafternoon. But midafternoon came and went and Brenna became worried. Around four o'clock she phoned Clay Sullivan.

Celeste answered. "Hi, Brenna! Clay told me you were in town."

She bet he did. Just what had Riley told his partner? "I suppose Clay told you that…that Riley and I have a baby."

Celeste was silent for a few moments, as if she didn't know quite what to say. Brenna knew the feeling. Brenna and Celeste had always been friendly, but not really friends, for no particular reason. They'd taken different classes. And Celeste had been close to Mikala and Jenny. Brenna's closest friend had been Katie Paladin. She'd heard Katie had bought the town's flower shop and she wanted to look her up. But she just didn't know if time would allow the renewal of their friendship.

Finally Celeste asked, "How would you like to come over for lunch? I'd love to catch up."

Celeste wasn't about gossip. She'd had enough herself. And Brenna knew the invitation was genuine, a hand reaching out. She felt ready to take it. "I'd like that, if you don't mind a baby fussing now and then."

"I love babies. Maybe we can do it sometime next week."

"That would be great. But Celeste, right now I need

to talk to Clay. I'm worried about Riley. He said he'd be back midafternoon and it's way beyond that."

"Hold on. I'll get him." There was an urgency in Celeste's voice that she'd picked up from Brenna.

Clay was on the line in seconds. "Hi, Brenna. I hear you're worried about Riley."

"I am. Do you know anything?"

"I've been following the Doppler radar. Storms have been swirling around Feather Peak all afternoon. I'm sure Riley and his group got caught in them. You know there's no cell service there or I'd know what was going on. We talked about getting a satphone. We just haven't done it yet."

If Riley had a satellite phone, she'd know exactly where he was and she wouldn't be this worried. "Is he in danger?"

"He was a Marine!"

"That's not an answer to everything," she said with frustration in her tone.

"Uh-oh. I can see he's already given you that line."

She blew out a breath. "Yeah, he has."

"Seriously, Brenna, Riley is usually prepared for anything, especially when he takes out a group. My guess is they'd either stay in Horsethief Canyon and hole up in one of the caves, or they might have gotten as far as my great-grandfather's cabin. Remember that one-room rustic place near the old copper mine?"

Actually she did. The old cabin had a woodstove and supplies for anyone who might need them. Once she'd become a decent rider thanks to lessons from Silas Decker and his son Zack on the Rocky D, she and Zack had ridden out to Feather Peak and other points of interest more than once. So much of the scenery on the outskirts of Miners Bluff was beautiful.

Even more than her rides with Zack, she recalled in detail her hikes with Riley up Moonshadow Mountain to Starfall Point. There they could see the valley below and really the extent of their world at that time. Those hikes had been an escape for her and Riley, too.

"How bad are the storms?"

Clay hesitated.

"Don't sugarcoat it, Clay. I know how fast they can move in over the mountains."

"Do you have an email address?"

"Sure." She rattled it off to him.

"I'm going to send you a link. Click on it. You'll be able to see the storm cell. Right now they're not as intense. But if Riley did stay holed up in Horsethief Canyon, it'll take a while to get out into cell range. And if the storms are coming through all evening and he doesn't have real experienced riders, he's not going to go anywhere until morning."

"So this could be a very long night?"

"Only if you stay up worrying. I don't see a reason to worry. He *does* know what he's doing. You have to trust him."

Trust Riley O'Rourke. Trust that he knew best, trust that he could take care of himself, trust that he'd be home safe. Those were an awful lot of trusts.

After Brenna thanked Clay, Celeste came back on the line. "Do you want me to come over and stay with you? If Feather Peak's getting sudden storms, they might come down through here."

"I don't want to pull you away from your family. I'll be all right, Celeste. Really."

"Did Riley show you his stash of oil lamps, batteries, that kind of thing?"

"No, he didn't. But I'm sure I can find them."

"Clay could bring over a few supplies and show you how to work the generator."

"Generator?"

"In case the electricity goes off."

"Derek and I don't need much. We'll be okay until Riley gets back. I can always light the fireplace."

"You know how?"

"You mean do I know how to do it without getting smoke all through the house? I think so. I haven't been away from Miners Bluff so long that I've forgotten everything I've learned."

There was a short pause and then Celeste said, "Riley will be fine. He's been through storms before."

Maybe he had. But none like the one they were going through now.

As night fell Brenna's concern deepened. *Was* Riley prepared? Had he taken along gear for an overnight stay? Was he in the canyon or somewhere else?

So many questions she didn't know the answers to. She did find two oil lamps. Fortunately she didn't need them, although thunder grumbled, lightning flashed and rain fell. Derek seemed oblivious to it all and she tried to be, too, holding him in her arms through much of the night to give herself comfort. When morning broke, she was glad to see the clouds had passed. Turquoise sky hosted a brilliant sun.

Finally around 10:00 a.m. she got the call that mattered—the call from Riley. She asked first thing, "Are you all right?"

Silence met her blurted-out greeting. "I just got phone service. We should be at the Rocky D in about half an hour."

She could hear voices, the clip-clop of horses, and now she wondered what she'd been so worried about.

Taking a deep breath and letting her panic roll away, she strove for a more neutral tone. "I was worried last night. I called Clay and he said you'd probably stay in Horsethief Canyon or in the cabin near the copper mine."

"You called Clay?"

"What was I supposed to do when you didn't come home?"

Again that silence. Finally Riley admitted, "I'm not used to having someone check up on me."

She couldn't tell if he was annoyed she'd checked up on him or pleased about it. But that was Riley, stoic at the most important times. Even more stoic now that he'd been trained not to let his feelings show. She understood that completely in war, but in real life it wasn't a benefit. "Did you get wet?"

"Not too bad. We did camp in Horsethief Canyon and stayed in one of the caves with a natural flue. We had a campfire and enough rations between all of us."

After a few awkward beats, she asked, "How about pot roast for supper?"

"You know how to make pot roast?"

"What is it with everyone? Do you think I went away to New York and had a personal chef?"

"I don't know what happens in your life in New York. You haven't really told me."

If she wanted communication, she'd gotten a little bit of it there. "I'll tell you when you get back," she promised.

One of his group directed a question at him. Riley said, "I've gotta go. I'll be home in about an hour."

An hour. To pretend she hadn't missed him. To pretend she hadn't worried about him. To pretend she didn't look forward to seeing him again. Because if she pretended, maybe she could act as if all those things were so. She stared at her phone, wondering why she cared so much. Because he was Derek's dad?

She certainly hoped that was the case.

When Riley came through the door, she fought the urge to run to him and throw her arms around his neck. Only significant others did that.

Lovers do that, a little voice in her mind reminded her. But she quieted it by taking one of Riley's saddle packs from him as he discarded other gear.

"Thanks," he said over his shoulder.

"No problem."

"The rest of this gear goes in the garage. I'll be right back." His gaze met hers. "It's been a very long time since a woman worried about me."

"I'll bet your sister does it all the time."

"Not the same." His voice said he was sure of it as he walked down the hall and slipped into the garage. Ten minutes later he was back.

"Are you hungry?" As a teenager Riley had consumed huge amounts of food. From what she'd seen so far, that hadn't changed.

"Yeah. Those granola bars were a long time ago. But you know what? You look more exhausted than *I* feel. Did Derek have a rough night?"

"No, but I couldn't sleep."

That must have put Riley's radar on red alert because he came right up to her. "Was the storm that bad?"

"Don't play a game with this, Riley. I was worried about you. I didn't know where you were, if you were wet or cold, if you were taking care of everybody else and not yourself."

He didn't seem affected by her outburst. "I wish I could have sent you smoke signals. But you have to be prepared when I go out on these trips that something like this might happen. The weather is as unpredictable as human nature. You can't lose sleep and worry."

"But I *did* worry. You're Derek's father."

His voice went lower and huskier. "Is that *all* I am?"

Riley smelled like outdoors and man. Sage and musky male were a potent mix. His T-shirt practically molded to him and his physical strength was a force to be reckoned with. But it was the attraction and pull toward him that worried her. She just wanted to crawl into his arms, tear his clothes off, touch him until she was filled up with him.

He wanted her to admit something she couldn't admit, not to herself, and certainly not to him.

Their staring duel ended when he swore, murmured, "Brenna, you make me nuts," and pulled her into his embrace. Their kiss was raw and hungry. Riley swept defenses away before she could even put them up. Their kiss stated irrevocably that he was a man and she was a woman and he wanted her and she'd better admit she wanted him.

Oh, she did want him—in that crazy, passionate way a woman fantasizes about. This was the one man who made her feel totally like a woman. But this was also a man who might have an agenda that could hurt her and maybe Derek, too. Still, she let him kiss her senseless and she responded with all the concern and worry that had plagued her through the night. She never wanted anything to hurt Riley, and for more reasons than the fact he was Derek's dad. They had a history. He'd been her first love.

Before she knew what was happening, they were on the sofa and he was lying on top of her. There was no doubt they fit together like a man and woman should.

Riley was on one elbow, stroking her cheek, running his hand down her knit top over her breasts. She reached for his shirt and almost tore it off as she sought to feel the skin underneath. His chest hair stopped her slide downward and she played in it awhile, making him groan. One of his legs was between hers and she rubbed against it as they kissed. It wouldn't take much—

Derek's cries froze any hot response she was about to have. Riley went still, too, and the moment became one of those awkward ones you never forgot. Like the one she'd escaped when she'd left without waking him the morning after their reunion. This one she wasn't going to escape. She'd been so hot for him that in another second she would have come. One look into his eyes and she knew *he* knew it.

She sat up as best she could, saying, "I have to go to him."

"He's crying, Brenna. He's not in any danger."

"That's not the way it works, Riley. When a child cries, a mother goes. No matter what."

"I can change him," he said, climbing off the sofa and getting to his feet.

"You have to get something to eat. I'll take care of him."

Before Riley could protest, she went to Derek, her eyes misting a bit at the turbulent emotions inside of her.

While Brenna nursed Derek, she smelled the aroma of bacon and wondered what else Riley was cooking. She'd lost her appetite after she couldn't get in touch with him and now her stomach grumbled at the aroma.

Brenna was changing her son when Riley came into the room, a glass of milk in one hand, a toasted sandwich on a plate in the other. "I'll take over with him. You eat."

"I can finish—"

"Brenna, I know you. If you were worrying last night, you didn't have an appetite and you probably didn't eat. You can't nourish our son if you don't get nourishment, too." He put the glass of milk and the sandwich on the nightstand, then took her place at the changing table. "Go on and sit. I'll walk him a little, then bring him back in. He can stare at the mobile for a while."

As a single mom she was used to jumping up in a moment, at having meals interrupted, sleep interrupted, anything interrupted. Knowing Derek was in Riley's care gave her a sense of relief that she could actually stare at the food and know she had the time to eat it. She took a bite of the lettuce, tomato, cheese and bacon sandwich and thought nothing had ever tasted better. She slowly chewed, then washed it down with a swallow of milk. She felt herself relaxing and didn't know when that had last happened.

By the time Riley returned with their son, she'd finished the sandwich and the milk and was just rocking back and forth, trying not to think about what had happened in the living room, trying to concentrate on the blue sky out the window and the sun glinting off the maple leaves.

Riley noted, "You look better already."

"Thank you, I guess."

He grimaced. "I'd better brush up on my man-woman repartee." He settled Derek in his crib and turned on the mobile, letting it spin.

A duck and a cat and a cow slowly chased each other around the circle. Derek seemed fascinated by the objects, even though Brenna knew it was too soon for him to focus. She expected Riley to leave the room, but he didn't.

Instead he went to the bed and stretched out on top of the spread, legs crossed at the ankles, arms under his head. "So tell me about *your* repartee."

"Excuse me?"

"Tell me whom you date and why."

"I don't date."

He gave her a skeptical look.

"Why you don't believe me?"

"Because you're one beautiful woman, accomplished, successful. Why wouldn't you go out?"

She stopped rocking, checked out his semirelaxed pose and took her first stab at trusting him. "I didn't choose very well when I did try to get serious."

"What happened?"

His question was even and conversational, as if it was no big deal.

As she studied Riley, she remembered secrets they'd shared. She'd told him about feeling smothered by her parents, how she'd felt on the outside of friendships, how she'd longed to get away from Miners Bluff. As far as she knew, he'd never turned any of those around on her, told anyone else or made her feel more insecure. This was the boy she'd thought about happily-ever-after with, yet had known it never could happen.

Could she trust him? She'd have to if they were going to parent together. That thought had her shaking in her proverbial boots.

But they did have to start somewhere. And Thad *was* almost ancient history.

When she gazed into Riley's eyes, there was reassurance there. So she began, "I dated a stockbroker, Thad Johnson, for almost a year and a half. I was a designer for Girard Bridals then. This was before I went out on my own. I was friends with another designer at Girard—Charlene. I shared an apartment with her to keep expenses down because I wasn't taking any money from Dad. I let him pay for school, but that was all."

She'd dropped her eyes to Derek while she was talking, but now she glanced at Riley again. He looked interested, curious even and she felt like a fool as she went on, "This is *so* clichéd." She really didn't want to tell him the rest.

"I'm not sure I know the meaning of that word, so tell me anyway." He was teasing her, trying to get her to lighten up. He'd always been able to do that.

"It still hurts, Riley." Maybe she hadn't known that before this moment, but right now she did. "I thought Thad and I were going to get married. We had looked at rings. And then one night that I had worked late but Charlene hadn't, I came home earlier than expected and found them together. Afterward Thad explained he was unfaithful because he didn't want to get married. That was his way out. But after I rented another apartment and we broke up, he married Charlene! Working beside her was so awkward. I was ready to step outside the boundaries of what I had done at Girard and that's when I went out on my own."

After a few beats of silence and Derek's little sighing noises, Riley said, "So the breakup turned into something positive for you."

She had looked at it that way, too. "I would have gone out on my own at some point, but yes, that was the impetus."

"You loved him?"

Now there wasn't any teasing in Riley's eyes, nor amusement, nor anything light. He wanted the truth.

"I don't know if I know how to love, Riley. I left you to be loyal to my family, to grow up and become a person in my own right. And Thad…maybe he was simply part of the dreams many young girls have—the white gown, the veil, the grill, the backyard and family. Dreams were tied into what I had with him."

"So he crushed your dream, and that's why it still hurts."

"Have you taken Psych 101?"

That brought a smile from Riley again as he sat up on the side of the bed, his knees almost touching hers. That trembling awareness was there, shifting into high gear. "Nope, no psych courses. But on a black night in a bunker guys talk, and there are lots of stories to share. Everybody has a dream to get them through tough times…to bring them home. I learned a lot about human nature."

She supposed he had. She could see it in the lines around his eyes, around his mouth, in the set of his shoulders and the jut of his jaw. "And what was the dream that brought *you* home?" It was suddenly very important that she know that.

He looked down at his boots and then back up at her. "Family. A place like this."

She'd expected those answers, but she'd also wondered about something else, just as he had. "So when did you last have someone special?"

He met her gaze unwaveringly. "Having someone special was tough when I was constantly being deployed."

Something in his voice alerted her. "But you tried?"

"I tried—a couple of times. But you know my opinion of women, Brenna. They don't stay when the times get tough. Times are tough when you have to wait for someone. Times are tough when a couple is in two different parts of the world. My last relationship was with a journalist and… I should have known better."

As soon as he said the words, he looked as if he wished he hadn't. He nodded to Derek. "I think he's settled in for the afternoon. And I think we've had enough soul baring to last us a year."

If Riley thought *that* was soul baring, he didn't know what soul baring was. They'd been trading experiences and romantic pasts, that's all. Maybe that's all the deeper the two of them would ever go…unless they were talking about Derek.

She'd let her guard down with Riley today. She'd let him see that she cared. And they both knew she didn't just care for their son's sake. She cared about Riley. But she would not fall for him again. She couldn't. Because this time if they broke apart, she might not be able to put her heart back together.

For the next week Brenna went her way and Riley his. His work commitments kept him away all day, sometimes into the evening. On her part Brenna worked when she wasn't caring for Derek, had lunch with Celeste and took Derek to visit her mom again. While her mother cooed over the baby, Brenna dodged any personal questions and came home more tired than if she'd spent a sixteen-hour day at the office or in her store. She wasn't getting enough sleep, but she didn't have time to sleep.

On Saturday night Riley received a late night phone call. His fishing trip for the next day had been cancelled. The family that had hired him had come down with the flu. So he was around on Sunday as Brenna handled Derek and work. Without making a big deal of it, he took over handling the baby so she could concentrate longer and better. He even cooked supper—roast chicken with mashed potatoes and fresh vegetables. As she sat down to dinner and baby-talked at Derek in his little swing, she appreciated everything Riley had done for her that day.

Her phone rang. She picked it up, saw that it was one of her assistants, then answered it.

After she'd finished and hung up, Riley asked, "Want me to warm your plate in the microwave?"

"No, it's fine. I was only on five minutes."

"More like fifteen."

They ate quietly, both of them talking to Derek, a tension between them that stemmed from being together in the same place…at the same time.

When their gazes connected, Brenna looked away. Riley was a little too quiet and she wondered what was coming. His care of Derek today, the nice dinner…

She braced herself.

Finally when he set a dish of berries in front of her with a dollop of whipped topping, she definitely knew something was brewing. She ate a spoonful, tickled Derek's foot, played with his little hands, made sure he was content.

"Brenna?"

There was that tone of voice that said Riley wanted to talk. She was almost afraid to hear what he wanted to discuss. "What?"

"Derek will be fine for a few minutes. I need to have a conversation with you."

"I'm right here, Riley."

"I need your attention."

"You've got it." She folded her arms over her chest, not even realizing it.

As she stared at him, he just shook his head. "You're not making this easy."

"*What* am I not making easy? Don't you think I had a feeling about this? You helped me with Derek all day, you made dinner, you even served dessert. That's not our usual day. Of course I think something's up. So, what is it?"

"We need to discuss joint custody. I want to know my son. I can't know him if I don't spend time with him. So whether you're in New York and I'm here, I still want that time."

She stood up from the table, all ready to gather up Derek and run.

But he stood, too, and clasped her shoulders. "Don't be afraid of this, Brenna. You can trust me with him. Can't you see that?"

"Even if I can trust you with him, I don't want to be away from him. I'm his mother. What are you thinking?"

Riley kept his tone even. "Possibly a long weekend to start. Then maybe a week. Then after a while, maybe two. Maybe I could take him for a month and then you'd have him for a month."

Panic made it hard for her to speak. "And what would you do when you work?"

"What are *you* going to do when you work?"

She was ready for that one. "I have day care lined up, a wonderful woman who's like a grandmother to him."

"And I have a family that would be glad to help out. If I need recommendations for sitters, Shannon and Sean have helpers they already use. Working isn't an insurmountable obstacle, as you know."

She was close to tears. "Riley, he's my baby."

Riley's voice was teeming with compassion. "I understand. Really, I do. And no matter how old he gets, he will always be your baby. That's the way good mothers feel. But I'm his dad, and we made this situation, and we have to make it right. So just think about all of this…because it's going to happen, Brenna. We'll have to compromise. But I will have my son some of the time and you'll have him the rest of the time."

The idea caused such turmoil she couldn't blink fast enough to keep tears from falling.

Riley took her into his arms and held her.

She rested her head on his shoulder as if she could find safety there. Yet she knew better…because Riley still might be the enemy.

Chapter Six

When Brenna's cell phone rang the next day, she grabbed it, hoping it was Riley. After feeding Derek at five, she'd fallen back to sleep. Riley had been gone when she'd awakened, and he'd left a note.

Gone to see a prof at Northern Arizona U. about planning to take a class to the Grand Canyon. Should be home by lunchtime.

He liked what he did, that was obvious to see. She hadn't been to the Grand Canyon in years. It would be terrific to go with him, to stand there on the lip, just taking in all the beautiful colors and textures.

Her mind quickly cleared of that possibility when she checked the screen and saw the caller was her father.

"Hi, Dad. What's up?"

"I'm sorry I missed you when you visited your mom."

"I'm sorry I missed you, too." Yet in some ways she'd

been relieved. She hadn't wanted to get into an argument about staying with Riley.

"Well, I'd like to see more of you while you're here, and I figured out a way to make that happen."

Uh-oh. When her father planned, she worried. "What do you have in mind?"

"Because of what you do, of course, you know that June is bridal month. I'm involved in a promotion here at the store and I thought you might like to help."

He'd piqued her interest. "What is it?"

"A store-wide bridal event beginning June 1. We have a registry for gifts now. Katie Paladin and her flower shop will be doing all the floral arrangements in the bridal department. I thought you might like to bring in a few gowns from your store in New York and get involved in the PR. What do you think?"

Many thoughts were racing through her mind at once. First of all, she would not neglect Derek in order to be involved in everything. On the other hand, Riley wanted to spend more time with his son. Maybe this would be a perfect way to help it to happen. Secondly, doing this would be great publicity for her brand. She might be able to pull in new customers for her father's store, not only from Flagstaff, but from Phoenix and Sedona. *Bridals by Brenna* was more well-known now. She could help hike up McDougall's profit line as well as her own.

"This would have to happen pretty quickly, I would guess."

"That's why I'd like to get started. We have almost two weeks. Why don't you come down here to the store."

"I have Derek."

"That's fine. Bring him along. I'd love to see him. I'm sure I can handle him in my office if you want to check over the bridal department. We can get this going, have your gowns shipped within a week, ready everything for our June 1 sale."

Her dad had always treated her like a princess and she loved him, in spite of everything. Maybe she could really connect with him again and convince him to make peace with Riley.

"It sounds like a lot of fun. I should be there in about forty-five minutes. Is that all right?"

"That works for me. See you soon."

Brenna hung up her phone, wondering what she was getting herself into.

Every time Brenna walked into McDougall's, a feeling of joy and excitement filled her. Holding Derek close to her in a sling against her chest, she whispered to him, "I grew up here."

And she had, chasing after her dad, following him from department to department, asking all kinds of questions as she grew up. She liked the perfume counter with all of its beautiful scents that faced customers walking into the store. There were jars and tubes of cosmetics and a whole world to explore. She *had* explored it as a teenager, even more than her parents would have liked. To the left of that display was the shoe department, and she had to admit, she liked shoes. Even as a little girl she'd find as many as she could in her size and slip them on. When no one was looking, she'd slide into the high heels and think to herself, *I'll wear these someday.*

Her dad had never believed in decorations for different seasons, not in the kind of tinselly way some stores did. Chandeliers hanging from the ceiling were classic. Each department decorated on its own and he left the managers in charge of that. Now she could see signs of the wedding event that he was planning. There were wedding bells sitting on the counters, cake toppers here and there, an antique car with a just-married sign positioned on a shelf.

On the left behind the shoes was the menswear department where Father's Day signs stood. She'd explored there for presents for her dad for birthday and Christmas as well as Father's Day. Women's wear swept across the back of the store. Her father knew women were the shoppers both for themselves and for others.

Bypassing the elevator, she started up the wide staircase and smiled. Those steps had always reminded her of something from *Gone with the Wind.* On the second floor she wandered through home furnishings and housewares finally stepping into her very favorite part of the store of all—the bridal salon. There were a few gowns on mannequins, several hanging on tasteful clothes trees made of brass and solid wood. Part of the department was devoted to mother of the bride and attendants' dresses, but she knew the essence of it was located through the archway into the lounge area where a round dais stood before her with a panel of six mirrors wrapped around it. This was where a woman stood to really see herself in a bridal gown. Her family sat in the chairs below to give their opinion.

Stopping to canvass one of the wedding gowns, Brenna spotted a huge placard on a stand that announced a bridal fashion show the first weekend in June. That really wasn't the place for it. It should be in the lobby of the store. Her father needed to extend the bridal promotion into every department, to bring customers in to register for anyone getting married, and he needed to—

"So what do you think, Daughter? Did you notice

your gowns over there?" He pointed to two on mannequins.

"I did. But this year's ready-to-wear line is even better than last year's. You need to update, Dad."

"This is Miners Bluff," he protested gruffly.

"That doesn't mean every woman who's getting married in Miners Bluff doesn't look through all the bridal magazines and know what this season's gowns look like. We've talked about this before."

"Yes, we have, and now that you're here for a little while, maybe you can convince me to make the changes you'd like to see."

She eyed him. "Did you just put those gowns on display today and you really have this year's gowns in the back?"

He laughed, and hung his arm around her shoulders. "Brenna, my dear, you give me credit for being much more devious than I actually am. I do have this year's gowns in the back, but I'm saving them for the bridal show." He pointed to the placard.

"Yes, and we have to talk about that, too."

His eyes twinkled. "We do, do we?"

He held out his hands to her and asked, "Can I hold him?"

Her father really hadn't had any time to spend with his grandson yet. Maybe she'd just taken it for granted that he'd be awkward with Derek, or not want to pick him up, or hold it against him that Riley was his father. But she didn't see any of that as her father lifted Derek from the little sling, and cuddled him in the crook of his very large arm.

"He's beautiful, Brenna," he said, his voice a little husky.

It was unusual for her dad to show emotion, but now seeing it, she felt a little misty-eyed herself.

"Why don't we go to my office," he said, "and we'll talk about all this. I told you I hired Katie Paladin to create a different atmosphere in here for the month of June—more lavish, more elegant. She'll be using her expertise with flowers for the bridal fashion show, too."

"You know, don't you, that having your models walk down that staircase to the first floor in the gowns would be awesome."

He studied her. "And why was it you went to New York and opened your own store instead of helping me here?"

"Because I needed a life of my own."

Angus narrowed his eyes and really looked at her, maybe as he hadn't for a very long time. They'd had argument after argument about this after she'd gone to the Fashion Institute. She'd been determined to make her way in New York and he hadn't understood her need for independence. But holding his grandson in his arms and assessing her attitude once again, he didn't argue with her or defend his position.

He just said, "I have a fresh pot of boiling water in my office. Your mother says you're into tea now, so I pulled some decaffeinated from the gourmet shelf. We can make one of those lists you're so famous for about how I can increase sales and bring in more business. Times are tough for a lot of people right now."

As they walked toward housewares, went down an aisle, and behind the department to his office, Brenna said, "And the first thing we have to do is try to make a wedding more affordable."

His eyebrows quirked up. "You design one-of-a-kind gowns and sell them for thousands of dollars!"

"But I also have an off-the-rack line. Many brides save much of their budget for their gown. Maybe we should figure out how to make that the centerpiece of a backyard wedding."

Angus shook his head. "I don't know if I'm up for this."

Brenna laughed because she knew better.

Losing herself in the project, Brenna discussed ideas with her dad who took turns walking Derek, cooing at him and generally making a fuss over him. Her father hadn't mentioned Riley or asked about him. Of course he hadn't asked her any personal questions, either, and she was glad about that. Maybe he wouldn't try to interfere. Maybe he'd let her and Riley work things out on their own.

Her cell phone played and she took it from Derek's diaper bag. A purse wasn't necessary when she carried all of his paraphernalia in a leather tote big enough for the kitchen sink.

"Work?" her father asked as she studied her phone's screen.

"It's Riley. Excuse me while I take this."

Her father gave her a really-do-you-have-to? look, but then took Derek from her arms and walked him over to the window that looked out onto the parking lot.

Brenna thought about leaving her dad's office for privacy but then decided she had nothing to hide. It wasn't as if she and Riley were going to say anything her father shouldn't hear.

"Hi, there," she answered, "What's up?"

"I'm home," he said as if that should mean something.

"What time is it?"

"It's 1:30. Where are you?"

"Oh my gosh! I completely lost track of time."

"Derek's with you?"

"Of course he's with me. Where else would he be?"

"I don't know. Where *are* you?"

Had Riley expected her to be at home when he returned? Had he expected maybe to have lunch together, maybe even feed and rock Derek since his schedule permitted it today?

"I'm in my dad's office. He asked for my help with a bridal promotion he's carrying on in June."

The lilt in her voice was met by silence. Finally Riley asked, "Did he just think this up, or was it something he'd planned?"

"It was already planned. The promotion starts June 1, and I have some ideas on how to spice it up."

"I imagine you do." Riley's voice was flat.

"Riley, what's wrong?"

"I thought you'd be here when I got home."

"I thought I'd be back. But this is part of running my business, too. My line and my gowns will have exposure from this month-long sale. I could have customers from Sedona and Phoenix as well as Flagstaff."

"This is about you selling gowns?"

"This" could be complicated over the phone, but she didn't want to go there with her father listening. "I'll be home in about forty-five minutes. Can we talk then?"

"We can talk whenever you'd like. I'm not the one postponing the discussion."

Her hackles rose. "I'm in the middle of something."

"Obviously." He paused for a moment. "Did you eat lunch?"

"I forgot about lunch. Dad had a few pastries brought in and I munched on those when we first started."

"Isn't Derek distracting you?"

"No, he's not. I fed him before Dad and I started.

He'll probably sleep as soon as I put him in his car seat to drive back."

"I wish you had left a note, Brenna."

"I'll remember that for the future." She didn't know what else to say.

"See you soon," he said abruptly.

"Soon," she agreed, not sure exactly what they were going to discuss when she got home. Her father? Riley's custody? Her independent streak? She put her phone away and when she looked up, her father was watching her.

"You know you can move back home anytime."

"I know, Dad, but that's not the answer."

"And living under *his* roof is?" Now she heard the anger in her father's voice. He'd been keeping a lid on it. All it had taken was the mention of Riley for it to ooze out.

"No arguments, Dad. It's not good for Derek and it's not good for me." She took her son from her father's arms and settled him once again in the sling at her chest. He was where he belonged.

"Brenna, why can't you see—"

"I don't know *what* you want me to see. Riley is a good man. He's a decorated veteran and you should see him with Derek. He's gentle and tender and caring."

"And how is he with you?" Angus asked as if he knew more was going on than sharing responsibility for their son.

"I'm not going to discuss me and Riley."

"I don't like this, Brenna. He could be leading you on to get what he wants."

"And what do you think he wants?"

"My guess is, he wants you to stay in Miners Bluff

with Derek. He also still might want revenge for what he thinks I did to his father."

"Sometime, Dad, we're going to have to talk about what *did* happen to Liam O'Rourke. You didn't just shut down his business. You shut down his life."

"Brenna—"

"Not now, Dad. Not here." She motioned to the list on his desk. "Show that to your managers and then we'll talk again."

He seemed to debate with himself whether or not he wanted to argue with her. But instead of arguing, he said, "We're going to really have to get into gear if we put a lot of these suggestions into practice."

"We can. I can have gowns here within a week, and anything else you might need, too."

"Can you set up a meeting with Katie?"

"I'll call her after I get back to Riley's."

Her father picked up the diaper bag and handed it to her, then he walked her past housewares to the top of the staircase.

In a low voice, so no one else could hear, he said, "If Riley isn't good to you, if there's dissention while you're living there, please come home."

She stood on tiptoe and kissed her dad on his cheek. "I'll call you after I talk to Katie." Without further discussion about her personal life, she blew him a kiss, gave him a wave and descended the stairs.

She'd just pushed open one of the two heavy glass doors and stepped into the sunshine when she recognized a woman reaching for the other door handle.

"Mikala?" Brenna asked.

Mikala Conti had been quiet in high school, though not shy. More than once she'd stepped up when she'd felt strongly about something. But for the most part, she'd kept her own counsel and had just seemed to take everything in. At the reunion Brenna had heard Mikala had become a music therapist who was thought of highly enough to have clients come to her from other parts of the country. At lunch Celeste had told Brenna that Mikala had married Dawson Barrett, another of their classmates.

Mikala laughed and gave Brenna a hug. "Hi there. I heard you were back." Mikala gently rubbed her fingers across Derek's head. "And who's this little guy?"

"Meet Derek Ryan McDougall."

"He's beautiful."

Brenna tapped Mikala's hand with the rings. "I heard you got married."

Mikala actually blushed a little. "Remember Dawson Barrett?"

"Oh, yes," Brenna said with a nod. "You did always look at him as if he was the best invention since chocolate cake."

"I did not!"

"You did. I'm glad to see it worked out. When did this all happen?"

"After the reunion. Dawson brought his son back here to live and, well, I wore one of your gowns for the wedding. I love your work, Brenna. It's beautiful."

"Well, thank you."

Mikala hesitated a moment, gazed at Derek, then back at Brenna. "I'm pregnant, too. Dawson and I can't wait to be parents, not only to his son Luke but to a new baby, also."

"When are you due?" Brenna asked.

"November. Everything kind of happened at once."

Brenna noticed Mikala didn't seem embarrassed about it at all. Maybe she should take a page from her friend's book. "I know what you mean. I never thought I'd be back here with Riley's baby."

"When love comes calling, sometimes a woman loses her good sense."

"Oh, this didn't have anything to do with love," Brenna quickly said. "I mean, it just happened the night of the reunion. Riley and I always knew we shouldn't be together, and I think knowing that just makes any chemistry more explosive."

"You and Riley weren't a secret in high school."

"Of course we were."

"Like you said, Brenna, another girl can tell the way a girl looks at a guy. I remember seeing the two of you duck under the bleachers for a kiss."

Brenna's hand went over her mouth. "Are you serious? And you never said anything?"

"It wasn't any of my business. Everyone knew about the bad blood between your families. I wasn't going to spill the romance between the two of you. I'm pretty sure Jenny knew about it, too. You'd painted an ornament for Zack to give his mom one Christmas. You *could* always draw and sketch and paint. You met Zack behind the Feather Peak Diner to give him the ornament. Jenny saw Riley pick you up. She mentioned it to me in passing and we just gave each other one of those looks and let it go."

"I'm grateful you didn't say anything back then. The lid would have been blown off our lives."

"So where's that lid now?"

Brenna guessed Mikala would have a good idea of what the complications were from Derek's birth. "The lid was blown off when we told our parents. But we're hoping for the best."

"Are you staying at your mom and dad's?"

"No, I'm staying with Riley. He deserves to get to know Derek."

"It sounds as if we all have some catching up to do. Maybe we can get together. I know I'd like some pointers about being pregnant…and afterward." She eyed Brenna. "You look great."

Brenna laughed. "It took work, and still does, but I love being a mom." She didn't know how long she'd been standing there talking with Mikala, but it was probably longer than she thought.

"I've got to get home now, though. Riley was expecting me to be there and I wasn't."

"First crisis?" Mikala asked.

"Heavens, no," Brenna said with a laugh. "And I'm positive it won't be our last." She fumbled with Derek's diaper bag, hooked her fingers inside, and brought a card out.

"Here's my cell phone number. Are you listed?"

"Both the studio where I see clients, and under Dawson's number. It was so good to see you again."

"We'll talk soon."

Five minutes later Brenna was on her way to Riley's house, hoping he understood her life was separate from his, even in Miners Bluff.

Feeling at loose ends, and that was strange in itself because he was *never* at loose ends, Riley sat at the computer in the alcove in his master suite updating weather charts, going over itineraries for upcoming tours, checking his schedule against Clay's. The first couple of weeks he'd been home after his discharge, he'd …ked, done ground work around his house, split logs …nerally found something to do for every waking …'d always been high-energy, never at a loss for what had to be done next. That had been an advantage when he'd joined the marines. Superiors had recognized those qualities and set him in the right direction.

But today when he'd returned home and Brenna hadn't been here, Derek hadn't been here, he'd felt… definitely at loose ends. He hadn't wanted to call her. She could have been at her parents, with friends, anywhere. But he'd just wanted to know where she was. He'd told himself she had his son with her and that's why he needed to know. But he missed her company. He missed the lilting sound of her voice, the baby talk she used with Derek, the scent of her perfume, her feminine presence in his house.

Stupid that he cared. Stupider still that he couldn't concentrate now. She'd said she'd be home and here it was, an hour later. His thoughts went to accidents, car trouble, a road block, road construction.

She was making him crazy.

When he heard the front door open, he made himself sit there calmly and count to five. Then he called, "Back here."

Derek was fussing when she came in, even though she cuddled him against her breast. He remembered what she'd said—*I don't want to be away from my baby.* Maybe a child and mother shouldn't be parted, especially at this age. But at what age *could* they be? At what age could Riley have his son all to himself?

"He was really good for me, but he began fussing in the car. I'm hoping if I dress him in some cooler clothes, and put him in that little swing we bought, he'll be a lot happier." She was at the door to his room and looked as if she didn't want to step inside.

"You can come in," he said, half teasing. "I won't bite.

Just lay Derek in the middle of my bed and see what he thinks of it. It's bigger than yours."

It certainly was. She had a double. He had a king-size. He never wanted to sleep in a bed again where his feet hung over the edge. He never wanted to sleep in a bed again that when he rolled over, he could have fallen off. As a big guy, beds and sofas and chairs were sometimes a problem…but not in this house.

Brenna laid Derek in the middle of the huge bed. Free from constraint, her son lifted his arms and legs, kicked and bobbled, cooed and gooed until they both smiled.

"Sometimes all he needs is a change of scene," she said.

"He had a change of scene all morning. So what were you doing at McDougall's? I mean, why did you go to begin with?"

If they were going to talk about her father, this could be a short conversation. He had to remember to listen more than talk, filter the noise and get the underlying message. Intelligence at its finest.

"It's not complicated. Dad called. He thought I could help with the bridal campaign. I could tell from his questions that he really liked several ideas I gave him."

"What's not to like? You learned from him. You have your own store and brides are your deal."

She laughed. "I think he came to realize that. So while I'm here, I'm going to work with him on this. The first weekend in June, McDougall's will have a bridal fashion show. I've convinced Dad to do a full ad campaign on the internet and in the local newspaper. I suggested he make a Facebook page and get the word out on other social media. There's no telling how far we could reach."

"Are you into all this?"

"I have to be. I have a virtual assistant who does most of it, and I have to manage everything we put out. So would Dad."

"Consultation has never been his strong suit," Riley muttered.

"No, it hasn't," she agreed easily. "But I think he realizes if we don't do something to reconnect again, there could be a real wall between us. I don't want that. I don't want to be the black sheep who did something wrong and now can never be forgiven."

"*Did* you do something wrong? Or did you just do something careless?"

"It doesn't matter, because Dad and I are going to get beyond it. We have to. I won't have another split like the one between your family and mine. I won't have a split between me and Dad."

"You wouldn't be split if I weren't in the picture."

"You're Derek's father. You'll always be in the picture. Whether you're in his life or out of it, you're going to affect him."

"So this idea of helping your dad—are you going to have time for it, what with your own work and Derek?"

"I'll make time for it. He wanted me to come back to McDougall's after I graduated to work with him. I didn't. So having a project like this now means a lot."

Riley could feel all the memories between them—the loyalties they'd always felt to their families that they weren't going to bring up again right now. Old feelings of resentment rose up as he thought about the years when his father was out of work, when he hadn't found Alcoholics Anonymous, when he'd cared about his buddies in the bar more than his own kids. But Riley realized that if he let those resentments rise up and if he dwelled on them, they'd just fester in his relationship with Brenna.

He definitely didn't want that. Yet somehow he had to figure out a way to get rid of them.

When Brenna sat on the corner of the bed, Riley pushed his chair away from his computer and went over to sit beside her.

She was looking at him as if she wanted to ask him something.

"What?" he prompted.

"It's none of my business."

"That never kept you from asking before."

She thought about that and then shrugged. "I'm just wondering if you've ever had anybody here to enjoy this with you." She motioned around the bedroom and to the bathroom with its whirlpool tub.

"I've never had anybody here but you Brenna. Shannon stuck her head in here a couple of times, but that's it."

"You've been without sex since the reunion?"

He laughed. "Why so surprised?"

"Because when we were together, we were always in the backseat of the car, or sneaking into your room, or something. I just always thought you were the type of man who—"

"Liked it a lot?" He laughed again. "Oh, Brenna. What about your Thad? Did *he* like it a lot?"

"That's not what we're discussing."

"So answer my question anyway. Did he?"

"If you're saying I wasn't sexy enough, if you're saying I didn't put out enough and that's why he was unfaithful—"

Riley took her hands which had started fluttering and held them as he kissed her lips. With their son lying on the bed, a kiss was all he was going to get…except maybe into deeper hot water with this conversation.

Brenna broke away. "See what I mean? And that's not the answer for everything."

"It answers a hell of a lot."

"Oh, Riley."

She rose to her feet and went to Derek who was still reveling in his new surroundings. "Come on, big boy, let's get you changed."

Drawing his own conclusions, Riley said, "So if you and Thad didn't spend much time in bed, what did you do?"

"We went to art exhibits, walked through Greenwich Village, went to the museums."

"No wonder you broke up," Riley said.

As soon as he said it, he knew he shouldn't have. Brenna gave him one of those I-don't-believe-you-said-that looks and left his bedroom.

Riley should have kept his mouth shut, or better yet, he should have just kept kissing her. Then he wouldn't have stuck his very big foot into his very big mouth.

Chapter Seven

The next day Riley came home to a house he didn't even know.

Katie Paladin and Brenna sat on the floor in the middle of the living room, sketches and photographs and magazine layouts spread across the braided rug. There were different types of flower arrangements on his coffee table and colored ribbons spread across one chair. A book of fabric swatches lay open on one side of Brenna and vases of different varieties and shapes stood in line to one side of Katie. To top it all off, Brenna's mom was pushing Derek around the room in his stroller. She looked as if she belonged there, as did the other two women. Brenna's mom having such a comfortable time in his home made him not only uneasy but resentful.

"Riley!" Brenna looked up at him as if he were the last person she expected to see, and that didn't make him feel any better than the rest of it. "I thought we'd be finished by the time you came home. What time is it?"

"It's five-thirty," he said gruffly, dropping his duffel by the door. "What's going on?"

The three women exchanged looks as if they were sending each other secret messages. He always hated that feeling when he walked into a group of women. Guys didn't do that, did they?

Katie explained easily, "This is about the sale at McDougall's. Brenna and I are coordinating our best ideas. I'm doing flowers for the whole store. Isn't that great? It will give Blooms so much more exposure. Maybe then townsfolk will realize we don't just arrange birthday bouquets or wedding treatments. We can do *anything*."

Riley knew Blooms's business was down like many other businesses. That's why Katie had been able to buy it. He was glad this would help her make a success of her new life here.

Brenna's mom wheeled Derek over to Riley. "I knew Brenna was helping her dad figure this all out, so I asked if she'd like me to come along to babysit. It's been great fun for all of us."

"I can see that." It had been a real women's day out, from the looks of it. That didn't make him feel any better about having Brenna's mom in his home.

Carol lifted Derek from the stroller. "Do you want to say hello to your daddy?"

Riley brushed his large hand over his son's hair, but he felt grimy and didn't know if he should hold Derek. "I've been out on the trail and feeling pretty dusty. I better get cleaned up first."

Carol looked up at him as if trying to see what his real intention in backing away was. He wasn't sure. He just felt totally unsettled and didn't like the prickly dissatisfaction that crawled up his spine. When he looked at Brenna, she looked almost happy. Why wouldn't she be? She had her work, her son and her mother close by. He just felt out of place in his own home and he didn't like it.

"I'm going to get a shower," he said, motioning to the master suite.

Katie was already scrambling to organize the photographs and pictures. "We'll probably be out of your hair before you come out of the shower. I'm filling in tonight at the shop."

Still holding Derek, rocking him as she walked, Carol commented, "Miriam will have dinner on the table at seven. I need to get changed and be ready for that."

Brenna gracefully rose to her feet and took Derek from her mom.

"If you're not here when I come out, have a good evening," Riley said politely before he went down the hall to the master suite and left the feminine chaos behind.

"He doesn't like me," Brenna's mom said to her as she gathered together her purse and sweater lying across a side table.

"That's not true," Brenna protested automatically.

"Oh, yes it is, and I don't understand why after all these years, he can't let it go."

Katie had always been a friend to Brenna and now was no time to leave her out of the conversation. She and Katie would be working closely and might have to deal with all of this together.

Brenna kept her voice low so Riley couldn't hear. "Do you and Dad realize what Dad did to the O'Rourkes so many years ago?"

Her mom swished the sweater around her shoulders. "I don't interfere in your father's business."

"This wasn't just business. This was a family's life that was ruined."

"I don't think I should be discussing this with you." She looked at Katie. "And not in front of anyone else."

But Brenna wouldn't be detoured. "We have to discuss this because the two families will be running into each other because of Derek."

"No one made Liam O'Rourke drink."

"No, but Dad pushing him out of his business caused enough stress to cause discord. It probably started with a few drinks as it always does, but then when his wife left, when the boys had to fend for themselves, when Liam fell deeper into depression and that bottle, their lives were never the same. I don't think you and Dad truly understand that. Sure, Dad had his reputation ruined, but it wasn't the same as what the O'Rourkes had to endure."

Her mother didn't seem pleased with Brenna's perspective as she asked, "Just how long are you staying with Riley?"

Brenna had planned on a month, but maybe she could swing six weeks.

Suddenly Riley was back in the room, his shirt unbuttoned.

"I left my duffel at the door," he said tersely, crossing to get it. As he did, silence filled the room. All three women watched him walk back to the bedroom.

After a sigh and a frown, Brenna's mother assured her, "Whenever you need me, call me. I'll be delighted to babysit. Any time I get to spend with my grandson is precious time."

"And don't feel you have to do everything alone,"

Katie added. "I have staff at the shop who can help, too. When are the dresses coming in?"

"In a few days. Grand opening date for the whole store for the bridal extravaganza is a week and a half away. I'm just hoping I can get the more comprehensive registries set up by then. They will help sales all around, I'm sure of it. I also made arrangements to bring Fulton Jewelry in so we have fine jewelry in addition to costume jewelry."

Her mom said, "It's about time we all band together and support each other's businesses. This was a wonderful idea, Brenna. And whether your father says it or not, I'm sure he's grateful."

"It would be nice to see Dad grateful rather than disapproving."

"Do you care if he disapproves?" her mother asked.

"I shouldn't, but I do. Don't daughters always care if their dad approves or disapproves?"

Katie looked away as if that concept bothered her dearly. Brenna hadn't had much time to talk with her alone, but they'd eased into their old friendship and she liked the feeling of that.

It didn't take long for Katie to gather her props and notes, telling Brenna, "You can keep the flowers. I don't know if Riley will care if they're here, but you can enjoy them."

Brenna gave Katie a hug. "It will be great working with you on this. I'm glad we're reconnecting."

Katie gave her an extra squeeze, then leaned away, smiled and nodded. "I am, too, and your baby is absolutely adorable. You are so lucky."

"Do you want one of your own?"

"I do, but I don't see that happening anytime soon. I'm not ready for another marriage."

Katie had married her high school sweetheart, a football star. She'd followed Ross to wherever his career had taken him. But then his career had ended and he'd later been killed in a sailing accident. The sadness in Katie's eyes told Brenna she wasn't over all of it yet. She'd only been back in Miners Bluff about a year, putting her life back together.

Brenna's mom said, "I'll help you carry some of these things to your car, then you'll only have to make one trip." She gave Derek a baby hug, then Brenna a tight mother-daughter hug. "Somehow everything will work out, honey. It always does."

"But not always the way we want it to," Brenna insisted.

When her mother gave her an odd, but knowing look, Brenna knew what it was for. She had to decide exactly what she wanted, what she could compromise on as well as what was best for all of them.

Derek was in his swing and Brenna was still straightening up a bit when Riley returned to the living room and remarked, "Everybody's gone."

"They would have been gone sooner if I'd been mindful of the time."

"It was jolting to come home to all this," he admitted.

Something had to be said to Riley about her mother, and now was as good a time as any. "Is that why you were so cold to my mom, because you felt jolted?"

She knew she should have picked her words more carefully when Riley's body stance stiffened and he looked ready for a confrontation. "I was polite."

"You were cold. That's not the way to win Mom over."

"Maybe I'm not trying to win her over. Maybe she

either likes me or she doesn't. Let's face it, Brenna, your parents never liked me."

"They never *knew* you. You're a man now, Riley, who served his country and has a job he's proud of. What's not to like?" she teased.

But her teasing didn't help. "This isn't easy."

"No, I know it isn't. But do you realize I finally got Isaac Fulton to take part in the sale with Dad? My father's invited him in on sales promotions before, but Mr. Fulton has always said no, mainly because he believed your father's rumors from years ago."

"They weren't rumors. Your father was greedy and ruthless."

Brenna sighed. "My point is, Mr. Fulton came around. It's time we all did. I think if you gave my mom half a chance, she'd give *you* one."

"I'll try to remember that," Riley said, tongue in cheek. "Were you and Katie hitting it off again?" He obviously wanted to change the subject.

"Yes. We got along great in high school. It's a shame what happened to Ross. I'd heard he'd settled into coaching and they had a good life."

"You never know. Plans can be disrupted in a day. Or in a night." Riley's gaze made a precise point as he crossed to the sofa, closer to her, then looked down at the coffee table at a photograph of a gown. "I don't know a thing about wedding gowns, but this is pretty."

"Only a man would call that gown pretty." It was a frothy, princess-style ballroom gown that most brides would love to wear. It was hanging in her showroom in New York and she was thinking about flying it in. It would be the centerpiece of all of her gowns.

He looked thoughtfully at the dress and then back

up at her. "Do you dream about wearing one of these sometime?"

"I don't need marriage. I know fairy tales don't come true."

"Are you against the institution of marriage, or committing to one man for a lifetime?"

"I don't have any problems with the institution, obviously. I make a living from it. I also don't have any problems with commitment. But I think the honesty, loyalty and faithfulness required for it are rare."

His arm was brushing hers. He smelled like soap and his hair was still slightly damp. If she ran her fingers through it now, they'd kiss. And if they kissed…

He must have been thinking the same thing, because he cleared his throat and stepped away. "I was going to take Derek to visit Dad tonight."

"I can go along."

Riley's raised brow asked his question for him.

"Just as I'd like you to get to know my mom, I'd like to get to know your dad. That's the only way we'll be able to put the feud to rest."

"I don't think it will happen," Riley said. "My father's too stubborn and your dad's too proud."

"But if he gets to know me, and finds himself attached to Derek, that could start changing things."

"And you think your dad and I will eventually see eye to eye?"

"We'll work on it," she said with more optimism than she felt. This had to work, or not only would their families stay divided, so would she and Riley.

She was beginning to realize she didn't want that at all.

Brenna was in her bedroom much later, studying sales reports her manager had sent her when she heard the noise. At first it sounded as if someone were beating against the metal shed in the back where Riley kept his tools. But then she thought she heard noises on the porch—clanging, rustling, something falling over with a bang. She was on her feet and standing protectively beside Derek's crib.

She looked out the window but, of course, couldn't see anything at midnight. So she went to the door and opened it.

Riley was coming out of his room, dressed in jeans but shirtless. "Stay put," he told her. "I'm going to check this out."

"That's not a good idea."

"I left gear on the back porch that I shouldn't have. Maybe it still smells like fish. It's probably just a little critter."

"Or a big critter. Black bears sometimes come down to the lower elevations."

"Did anyone ever tell you you worry too much?"

"Did anyone ever tell *you* you're reckless?"

He didn't seem to like that comment at all, but he didn't take time to stand there and argue with her. She heard his bare feet on the wood floor, heard him go out to the kitchen. He wouldn't go outside without any shoes, would he?

From her window at the side of the house, she could see light come on. That was the light outside at the sliding glass doors. She heard a clink, heard Riley open the glass doors and prayed he'd taken some kind of weapon with him.

Glancing at her sleeping son, she wished *she* could sleep so soundly.

A few minutes later Riley was back, standing at her doorway again. "It was a mule deer. No harm done. I should know better. It knocked over the poker from the outdoor fireplace and one of the chairs."

"I'd forgotten about the wildlife here," she said. "That takes some getting used to. I don't expect to hear things go bump in the night."

"Oh no, not many bumps at all, just sirens and garbage trucks and horns blaring. How do you ever sleep there?"

"And how do you ever sleep here with the silence?"

They were taking their corners again and she didn't want to do that. "We've got to stop comparing. One isn't better than the other."

"But you prefer the city noises now."

"That's my life, Riley, just as yours is trekking into the wilderness with Clay or tourists or whoever needs a guide."

He shifted from one foot to the other. The unsnapped waistband of his jeans slid a little left, then slid a little right. Her gaze went to the whorl of hair around his navel that she explicitly remembered touching.

Riley didn't leave but rather said, "I've been thinking about McDougall's sale and your part in it."

"It's important for me to help my dad."

"I realize that. Whether I like it or not, it's something you have to do. I do get that. So…I'll cover for you with Derek while you work on the sale. I want you to be able to depend on me…to learn to trust me."

"Are you offering so I'll agree to joint custody? Because one doesn't necessarily have anything to do with the other."

"We need to think about Derek first and what's best for him. I think that would be joint custody."

When she began to protest, he held up his hand to stop her. "But I also know I don't want to tear you away from Derek, or Derek away from you. It would have to be a gradual process. So how about starting with leaving Derek with me tomorrow while you go in to the store?"

"Leave him with you all day?"

"Do you want me to be insulted?"

"You can probably do it, but do you *want* to?"

"I do. I'm not going to take him horseback riding or kayaking or fly fishing. We'll just have a guys-day here, though I might take him out on the porch."

He was making all of her fears sound silly, but they didn't *feel* silly. Yet if she didn't do this, what would that say about her ability to compromise, to try to rebuild trust between them.

"All right," she decided, knowing she had to take this leap of faith.

Riley's face broke into a grin, "You made the right call."

"I'll know if I did or not tomorrow. I might be calling you every half hour."

"Call whenever you'd like. You might want to make a schedule for me. I know my sister likes to be consistent with Jakie."

"That's a good idea."

"I have a lot of them," he said with a wiggle of his brow.

She pushed on his chest lightly so he wasn't standing quite as close. Temptation was more easily eluded when it was farther away. However, as she touched him, his skin was hot under her fingers and she couldn't seem to pull her hand back, couldn't seem to do anything but stand there and stare at his black chest hair.

He folded his hand over hers. "We're hot together, Brenna, always have been and always will be."

It was fine that they were hot, but what else were

they? Living here was pushing her to try to figure out all that. Now she did snatch her hand back, went over to the dresser where she'd laid a notepad and pen.

"I'll make that list," she said brightly. "I won't have to leave until about eight, so I can feed Derek before I go. But I'll make sure there are bottles in the fridge."

Riley looked…frustrated. She was feeling a little frustrated, too. The problem was, what they would have to do to lead them out of that frustration could complicate their lives even more. She didn't want to deal with more complications. She just wanted to live with the one she had.

Riley obviously sensed her withdrawal, obviously sensed she wanted him to leave. But he didn't leave without twitching her ponytail, without giving her a wink and saying, "See you in the morning."

Riley didn't know how Brenna did it!

She'd left after Derek's second feeding this morning. Riley had thought the day would be fairly easy. After all, he'd helped take care of his niece and nephews. He had Brenna's schedule.

But…

An infant didn't care about the schedule and required more than feeding and a diaper change, and he didn't sleep all the time as Riley expected he might. He'd no sooner bathed Derek—which had scared the bejesus out of him because he was afraid he'd drop him—than the baby needed to be fed again. Okay, maybe the bath had taken a little bit too long. Then after he'd been fed, he was fussy and had to be rocked and walked. After he'd been rocked and walked, he'd had to be changed again. Not to mention there was laundry that had piled up, lunch skipped and a whole lot of crying in the afternoon.

How in the hell did Brenna do it? he asked himself again. Maybe he just didn't have her magic touch. And he'd thought joint custody would be a cinch? Caring for an infant would be a cinch?

When Brenna had called in the middle of the afternoon and asked how everything was going, he'd replied nonchalantly, "I've got it under control." If she needed more time at the store, fine.

But it wasn't so fine. He hadn't even thought about supper, and after her day at work, she'd need something hot, too. So he did something he never thought he'd do. He called his dad at the Shamrock Grill.

Riley had settled Derek in his swing and for the first time today, he actually seemed content. When his father came on the line, Riley asked, "What's the special today, Pop?"

"Why do you want to know what the special is when you're there and I'm here?"

He didn't need his dad being contrary. "I'm thinking about driving in and picking up two dinners."

"Brenna doesn't want to cook?"

"It's not just Brenna's job to cook," he snapped.

His dad went silent, then asked, "What's wrong, Riley?"

"Why do you think anything's wrong? I just want to know what the special is."

"I've spoken to you in the middle of war and you haven't sounded this rattled. So what's going on? Did Brenna go to New York and leave Derek with you?"

"She'd never do that," Riley muttered, sure of it. It would take an act of Congress to push her into joint custody. Maybe after today he knew the reason why. Moms and infants went together.

"So then what's the problem?" His father seemed to be getting impatient.

Riley knew the restaurant was probably full and his dad had a lot to oversee there. He hadn't wanted to tell his father about this, but maybe it was time they all stopped walking on eggshells. Maybe it was time for both families to look at the whole situation with a lot of honesty and perspective.

"McDougall's Department Store is having a bridal thing. So Brenna went in to the store today with her dad to work on it. I told her that was fine and I'd take care of Derek. But things got out of hand and I don't think I'll be able to cook supper, too. No big deal, Dad."

Again there was silence until his father asked, "So the bottom line is, in a backhanded way, you're helping Angus McDougall with his store?"

"Pop," Riley said exasperated. "That's not the way to look at it. Watching my own son is something I want to do. It also happens to help Brenna with something she wants to do."

"And you're trying to get something in return?"

"Maybe," Riley admitted reluctantly. "I'm trying to cooperate with her. If we're going to be parents together, we have to get along." Though there was getting along and there was getting along, he realized, reliving their passionate kisses, reliving the feel of her in his arms.

"So what time will she be home?"

"In about an hour."

"I've got three specials today—meatloaf and mashed potatoes, ham and green beans and chili. Take your pick."

Brenna had told him she couldn't eat certain foods because of breastfeeding. Better to stay away from spicy and salty. "Two meatloaf dinners would be great. I'll drive in and pick them up as soon as I can get Derek changed and—"

His father cut in. "I'll bring them out."

"I know you're busy. You don't have to do that."

"This isn't just a matter of you getting two dinners. I want to talk to you and Brenna about something."

Uh-oh. Riley didn't like the sound of that. But he really had no choice. If his dad was determined to do something, he'd do it, now or later. They might as well get it over with now.

An hour later when Brenna came home, Derek was crying again. Riley just couldn't seem to do anything right to satisfy him. Rocking or walking quieted him for a few minutes, but then he got fussy all over again. Riley had to admit, he was relieved to see Brenna walk through the door.

The thing was…she looked frazzled. In spite of that, over Derek's crying, she asked, "How was your day?"

He didn't answer her. He didn't have to with the baby crying because all her attention was on Derek. However, he had to give her credit, she stopped before she grabbed their son out of his arms.

"Do you want me to take him?" she asked.

"Sure," he said casually, as if it didn't matter at all. When she'd gathered Derek to her, he still wouldn't stop crying.

"Has he been like this all day?"

Moment of truth. "Most of it," Riley admitted. "I didn't want you to worry, so I didn't say anything when you called."

She went over to the sofa, pushed her hair out of her eyes, then laid Derek on his tummy on her lap. She drew circles on his back over and over again and he started to quiet.

"You didn't teach me that trick."

She tossed Riley a weak smile. "That's because I didn't think of it. I'll have to write everything down in a notebook, then when you babysit, you'll have it."

Babysit. He didn't just want to be a babysitter. He wanted to be a *father*. Gathering up the towel he'd laid here, a bib he'd laid there, an extra onesie he thought he might change Derek into if he went to pick up dinner, he asked Brenna, "So how was your day?"

"Hectic."

"Hectic how?" After all, he didn't know exactly what she was doing for her father, or what was involved in the sale.

"I had meetings this morning with Dad's department managers, then I had to talk to his network guru to see if he could get the registry set up fast enough."

"Registry?"

"Before Dad had the registry limited to china and silver and that kind of thing. But I wanted to make it a storewide registry which makes so much more sense. A couple could want something really odd for a wedding gift and it could still go in the registry, as long as their list is on their page."

"Page? You mean like a social networking site?"

"Sort of. A couple could do thank-yous from there for every present, have a wish list, anything they want. Dad really liked the idea, but actually getting it accomplished is something else."

"So you had meetings all day?"

"Well, no. I actually rearranged the bridal department, chose the gowns for display, phoned my store to make sure everything would be shipped in time. On top of that I had to handle phone calls about orders in my store that I usually take care of."

She was juggling a lot and she was quieting Derek, too. "You might be nominated for Woman of the Year."

When he said the words, he meant them as a compliment, but Brenna's face fell. In fact, if he was reading her right, she was close to tears.

He would have sat on the sofa beside her and asked her what was going on, but his dad arrived. He heard the truck in the driveway and then his father was knocking on the door.

Brenna looked down at Derek and concentrated on him, making those circles on his back even faster when Riley called to his dad, "Come on in."

His dad was carrying a large bag. He smiled at them both. "Two meatloaf dinners and I added two pieces of cherry pie. You ought to eat it while it's hot. Do you want me to take the munchkin?"

His father's use of the term made Brenna smile. Maybe Riley had been all wrong about her being close to tears.

"He's been fussy all day," she told his dad. "Are you sure you want to deal with that?"

"I had fussy kids. Patrick was the worst. Still is." He handed Riley the food and then opened his arms for the baby.

When Brenna was sure Liam had Derek on his shoulder securely, and to Riley's amazement Derek still was quiet, they took the containers of food into the kitchen.

Liam stood and walked with Derek while she and Riley sat at the table.

"You sure you don't want to join us?" she asked him. "There's more than enough here for three."

"That's because I wanted you to have leftovers."

She sent him a grateful smile and Riley realized she

could get along with his dad without a whole lot of extra effort.

As they dug in, she seemed to be as hungry as he was.

His father stood at the head of the table. “I know Brenna’s not going to be here real long, so I want to make a suggestion. I’d like to have a gathering at the Shamrock Grill to celebrate Derek’s birth. We can invite all our friends and family so they can get to know him. Not this Sunday, but maybe next Sunday?”

Brenna put down her fork. “That’s really generous of you.”

“Sure is, Pop.”

Brenna glanced quickly at Riley and he suspected what that was about. Would this be an opportunity for their families to take a step toward each other?

Riley didn’t particularly want to be around Angus McDougall, but the man was Derek’s grandfather.

“Pop, and I don’t want you to fly off the handle, but did you think about asking the McDougalls to this celebration?”

Riley watched as his dad glanced at Brenna and then his face turned a little ruddier. “No, I didn’t think about it.” His voice was clipped as if Riley should have talked to him about it one-on-one. But Brenna was involved in this, too, and it was time all of it was out in the open instead of hidden behind family names.

“I want you to think about it, Dad. Maybe it’s time we all moved forward.”

Derek suddenly seemed to wake up with the charged atmosphere in the kitchen. He began wiggling and then crying.

Brenna stood immediately. “I’ll take him. I haven’t been with him all day and I missed him. You and Riley can talk.”

And before Riley could remind her she hadn't finished eating, she'd left the kitchen and gone down the hall to her room.

He and his dad stared at each other. This was going to be one short conversation.

Chapter Eight

"Is he hungry?" Riley asked as he came into the living room and saw Brenna shifting Derek from one shoulder to the other.

It was almost midnight and Brenna was exhausted. She'd been rocking, pacing and swinging the baby ever since she'd gotten home. He was fussy and unsettled and she wondered if he was catching her mood. She'd been going since his first feeding that morning, but she knew resting was out of the question. She had a baby to take care of.

Riley had been on his computer, scheduling tours for the next week, trying to make phone calls between Derek's crying spells. He'd watched Derek all day so she didn't want to ask him to take over now. Besides, when she went back to New York, she'd be on her own again.

"I just fed him an hour ago," she answered Riley. "I

don't think that's it. And I just changed him again. He's just…not having a good day."

"He's having a different day," Riley said over the baby's wail.

Brenna shot him a quick glance.

He shrugged. "He was in a routine. You were here taking care of him, then suddenly today it's me. Maybe he didn't like the change in schedule."

"Babies are flexible," Brenna said loudly, trying to convince herself of it over Derek's new cry.

"Tell that to Derek," Riley shot back with a grimace. "Why don't you call Shannon? Maybe she could suggest something."

"It's midnight."

"She's my sister, Brenna. She won't care. Do you want me to call her?"

Brenna just kept walking and rocking and cooing, but she felt close to tears. She knew part of that was sheer exhaustion. But the other part—living with Riley, trying to be a mom, trying to work, trying to be a good daughter—were all stacking up.

No stress there, she thought, really wanting to just scream like Derek.

Riley plucked the phone from its stand and went to the bedroom. Brenna knew he was calling Shannon. He was a former marine—he didn't wait…he acted. If Shannon had the magic cure, she'd take it. She just hadn't wanted to admit she couldn't cope…couldn't handle it all.

She blinked fast, knowing Liam's visit had stirred up a hornet's nest, too. Just imagining her parents and Riley's family in the same room made her practically break out in hives.

Riley was shaking his head when he came back into

the living room. "She asked if you gave him a warm bath."

Brenna said, "Already did that. I tried the bear, too. Nothing is working."

"The only thing Shannon could think of was to try some music."

Music? Brenna *hadn't* thought of that.

"Come on," he said. "I'll wheel the crib into my bedroom. What do you think he'd like? Irish folk songs? Dad gave me a CD last Christmas."

"We can try anything." She really didn't care. She just didn't want Derek to make himself sick.

In no time at all Riley had pushed the crib into his bedroom and switched on his CD system. Then he took Derek from her arms and pointed to the bed. "Rest."

"I can't with Derek crying like this."

"Only one of us has to walk him at a time. Rest. If he doesn't quiet down, I'll hand him back to you."

He'd brought the wooden rocker in, too, and now he sat in it, laid the baby on his knees as Brenna had done earlier and rubbed the little boy's back in time with the music.

Derek cried for another five minutes, and Brenna was ready to hop up, grab him and try feeding again. But then his cries lowered in volume. As the music played, his whimpers subsided. Riley rocked and Derek seemed to relax with him. Before long, all was blessedly quiet.

Brenna sat on the side of the bed, not wanting to make a sound, not wanting to get Derek started again. With the worry of a new mom, she felt the weight of the responsibility she had toward her son and tears threatened again. Quickly she ducked her head so Riley couldn't see. She couldn't seem to stop the welling of emotion.

Gently without a sound, Riley lifted Derek into his

arms, stood and carefully laid him in the crib. Their son seemed to be sound asleep. The music had lulled him into peace.

After a moment of hesitation Riley sat beside her on the bed. “What's wrong?” he asked.

She would not let him see her cry. She would *not*. She shook her head.

He dropped his arm around her shoulders. “Brenna, come on. Talk to me.”

All of her doubts spilled out. “What if I'm not a good enough mother? Am I really going to be able to keep my career going? If I cut my hours, what will happen to the progress I've made in the industry? What if my day care falls through?” The questions seemed important and monumental, and she didn't have any of the answers.

His fingers stroked her arm. “You're tired right now, and everything looks bigger than it should. Of course you're going to be a good mother. Why wouldn't you be?”

She didn't want to answer, but she knew she had to put it into words. Her voice was low. “I don't know. Maybe I'm too selfish. I know I have to put Derek first, no matter what. But how do I balance that with what *I* need, too? How do I balance that with working and making a life for us?”

He nudged her into his shoulder. “You'll figure it out. *We* can figure it out.”

“What would have happened if you hadn't been here tonight? What would have happened if you hadn't called Shannon?”

“You probably would have walked with Derek all night, or taken him for a drive…or *something*. You're resourceful, Brenna. Today I think you just got a little overwhelmed. After all, in addition to everything else, you've taken on this sale of your dad's."

When she stiffened, he leaned away. "Now don't get defensive. You know it's a lot more than you planned on while being here."

That was true. Just dealing with Riley and their situation would have been enough, let alone keeping up with what was going on in New York.

They hadn't had a chance to talk since his father had visited, but if he could bring up her dad, she could bring up his. "So what do you think about what your dad wants to do?"

"You mean a celebration at the restaurant?"

She nodded, leaning into his shoulder again, feeling the comfort of his heat that was so much more than comfort, too.

"I think it's a fine idea. But if he decides to ask your dad, I don't know how that invitation will go over."

They sat there in silence a few minutes until Brenna said, "I never really knew your dad. I only knew about… the rumors."

"Alcohol changes a person. It changed him. We pretty much didn't have a dad for a lot of years. He'd checked out."

"But that's not true any longer. He's really turned his life around, and he seems very…caring. I admire someone who can do what he's done."

"He had to work hard at it. It wouldn't have been so difficult if he hadn't had to start over a second time."

Pushing away from Riley, she straightened and gazed straight into his eyes. "Do you blame *me* for what happened with our families?"

"If you really think about it, our parents' problems really have nothing to do with us."

She wasn't so sure about that. Their parents' problems were all tied up in their relationship, too.

Slipping off his shoes, Riley stretched out on the bed and opened his arm to her. "Come here."

"Riley, what are you doing? I can't stay here."

"Sure, you can. You need rest. I'll get up if he cries again. We'll both watch over him tonight."

There was tenderness on Riley's face and compassion, and she wasn't going to look for anything else. He looked so sexy and strong, stretched out on his bed, his arm open to her. They'd had a night in this bed. She remembered every detail of it. But tonight he seemed to be offering her something different, something she needed much more than sex.

"Come on," he said. "If you're not comfortable here, you can always leave. But I think this will be easier for all of us."

"At least for tonight," she murmured, settling down beside him.

He smoothed her hair back from her brow.

"You're a good mom, Brenna. There's no doubt about that. You just have to figure out how to piece it all together. I'll have your back, I promise you."

Brenna didn't know if Riley had ever made a promise to her before. Looking into his blue eyes, hearing the sound of his deep voice, wanting to believe with all her heart it was so, she took his hand and she closed her eyes, finally relaxing for the first time that day. She also let herself feel Riley's fingers curled around hers…let herself think about not doing all of this alone.

A tiny sound from the crib next to Brenna's side of the bed awakened her. She had become attuned to every sound Derek made. This one could be just a little huff because he was going to go back to sleep again, or it could turn in to a whole waking up routine that would require feeding, a bath and the start of their day.

Awake now, she realized exactly how she was sleeping. Riley was turned toward Derek and she was nestled against him. His long strong arms were around her as if she might escape while they were sleeping. How had this happened? When she'd fallen asleep, she'd barely been touching his hand, but now—

Derek whimpered, let out a little cry, and she wanted to scramble away from Riley before he woke up and found them that way.

But it was apparently already too late. As she started to slide away from him, his arm squeezed a little tighter.

"Don't be in such a hurry. I might like to wake up like this every morning."

He could be a charmer, he really could, and she'd fallen for that charm early on, with all the blarney that went with it.

Don't go there, she told herself, *just don't. If you're going to be parents together, you have to work at it together, not sleep at it together.*

Since Derek's cries were growing louder, she had the perfect excuse. "Thank you for getting up with him in the middle of the night. I really appreciated that. But now I'll get him. Sleep as long as you want. Last night meant a lot to me, Riley. It really did."

When she slid away from him, he levered himself up on his elbow. "If we had done something, what you said might have meant a little more."

"Riley." It was a scolding and he knew it.

He grinned at her anyway. "Just a suggestion, Brenna. Two people can do more than sleep when they're in bed together."

At the side of the bed now, she stood and went to Derek. "Yes, they can. But when they do, it can cause a mess of trouble. We know that, don't we?"

Now his grin vanished. "Is it so bad being here with me?"

She could never be anything but honest with Riley O'Rourke. "No, it's not bad. Sometimes it's very good. But you don't trust me or my family."

"You all want to keep your own close to you. I understand that."

Before they stepped into argument territory, she changed the subject. "Derek has an appointment with the pediatrician this morning for his hepatitis shot and a checkup. Are you taking out tourists today?"

"No, not today. What time—"

The phone at Riley's side of the bed rang and she arched a brow at him. "Kind of early."

"My brothers are early birds. Shannon can be, too. It could be anything from a car that wouldn't start to needing a babysitter."

After he answered the phone, he held his hand over the receiver and told her, "It's Patrick."

"I'll take Derek into my room and feed him."

"I won't be on that long. Guys usually aren't," he joked.

She shook her head at him and took Derek into the other room.

Riley didn't know why he liked to tease Brenna, probably to get a rise out of her. He liked to see those green eyes flash. He liked to see her look all indignant as if she wanted to stand right up to him and punch him in the nose. But then, of course, he'd kiss her instead. At least that's the way he saw it. Holding her last night—

That had been an experience he'd like to repeat. But

she was obviously having no part of it. She thought it would complicate their lives even more. He was of the opposite opinion. It might make their lives a lot easier.

When they were in the same state, that was. Ex-high school sweethearts with benefits?

"So Patrick, what's up?"

"You. We haven't seen you for a month. How about meeting me and Sean at the Tin Pan Tavern tonight? We can have a few drinks and catch up. I hear with *you,* there's a lot to catch up on."

Riley had been expecting this, dreading this, knowing he and his brothers wouldn't agree on many issues. "I can't do it tonight," he said. "I want to spend as much time with my son as I can."

Strained silence met his response. Finally Patrick asked, "What's happening to you, Riley?"

"*Nothing's* happening."

"Do you even know for sure he's *yours?*"

Riley wanted to shout, *Yes, he's mine.* But his brother wouldn't accept his gut instincts. "We should have the results of the DNA test soon."

"I don't get why you won't meet us. So now when Brenna's around, we can't get anywhere near you?"

"That's not what I'm saying," Riley insisted, annoyed yet keeping his tone even. "In fact, why don't the two of you come over *here* like Shannon did? You can meet Derek, we can order in pizza, we'll have a nice night. We can even play some poker."

"With Miss High-and-Mighty raising her nose and acting like she's better than us?" Patrick's voice was filled with the disdain his whole family had once felt.

"Brenna's not like that," Riley protested. "She never was. You were ahead of her in high school, so you didn't know her. Sean was two grades lower in high school so he didn't know her. Have you talked to Shannon?"

"Oh, Shannon bonded with her because they both have kids. That shouldn't enter into it. Her family made our lives hell."

"No." Riley was adamant. "Dad's drinking made our lives hell."

"Mom didn't leave because he was drinking. He wasn't heavy into it then. She left—"

Riley cut in. "She left because she didn't want to stand by dad while he got back on his feet. She left because she didn't want to be married to a short-order cook rather than the owner of a restaurant. She left because she was tired of taking care of *us*."

"You don't blame Angus McDougall for what happened to our family? Are you crazy, Riley?"

They had never talked about this out in the open before. The feud had been the gorilla in the room, but never spoken about. Well, now it was going to come out. All of it.

"Do you and Sean want to come over tonight and broaden this family a little? Don't you want to meet my son?"

"Not while Brenna's there. And I know I speak for Sean. We feel the same about this. You'd better watch it, Riley. The McDougalls think they're entitled to anything they want. Angus feels entitled to being a big man in town and doing what he wants because of it. Brenna feels entitled because she left, made a name for herself and probably has as much money as her father. And because of that she's going to feel entitled to your baby. Don't think being nice to her is going to change any of it."

No amount of coaxing, scolding or just plain getting

angry would change his brother's mind. Patrick's attitude toward the McDougalls had always been bitter. But on top of that, he'd had a rough divorce. He only had limited time with his sons now and he resented that fact, too. Riley felt sorry for his brother but knew Patrick had to find his own happiness.

By the time he went to find Brenna, she was sitting in the rocking chair in her room, still feeding Derek. She'd covered herself, expecting him to come in. It was strange. He wanted to watch his son suckle at her breast, and not in a sexual way. He wanted to watch because Brenna was so natural with him and he got this weird feeling in the pit of his stomach when he saw them together.

She apparently thought folding a blanket so he couldn't see Derek at her breast would save them both embarrassment. But he was still imagining how she'd look without that blanket.

When she saw his face, there must have been some sign lasting from his frustration with his phone conversation because she asked, "Is everything all right?"

Just how much should he say? He didn't want to feed any bad feelings she had about his family, but he couldn't just gloss over them, either.

"Patrick and Sean need their heads knocked together," he admitted.

Her eyes widened in surprise. "That's an unusual statement coming from you. You love your brothers." But as soon as she said it, she knew. "Oh, me staying here. Riley, what can I do? Maybe we could invite them over."

But Riley was already shaking his head. "I tried that. They won't come."

"They'd rather feed old bitterness instead of trying to find a reason to get along?"

When her voice shook a little, Riley hurt for her. This wasn't her fault any more than it was his.

He crossed to her chair and tried to put the best face on it. "I believe they think they're being loyal."

"To your dad?"

"To my dad, to the O'Rourke name, to some kind of family code that says we should stand together and fight for what is right for all of us."

"But what *is* right? What are they fighting for? What do they want?"

"You got me. I don't even think an apology from your father would do it."

"An apology from my father?"

Uh-oh. He'd stuck his foot in it again. "You know what I mean, Brenna. Just some sort of admission that what he did ruined my dad's life."

She looked as if there were a thousand words on her tongue and she was carefully not saying any of them. After what must have been fifteen deep breaths, she did say, "And is your father going to apologize to mine for ruining his reputation?"

Riley was about to rebut that when he suddenly knew better. That was exactly what had kept rubbing salt in the wounds all these years.

Hunkering down, he pushed a few tendrils of hair from her cheek. "Seeing us together sends my brothers a message they don't like, but there's nothing we can do about that. Sean's wife will be more likely to see our point of view, then maybe Sean will, too. And Patrick..." He shrugged. "When everyone sees that you and my dad can be friends, and you and Shannon can relate, maybe then they'll understand that this isn't about the past, it's about the present and the future."

Whatever defensiveness had risen up in her seemed to evaporate. "Do you really believe that?"

"I do."

She went very quiet as if she was debating about what she was going to say next. "And how do *you* feel about my father."

Riley stood again and measured each word. "I don't know your father. I only know what I've heard about him. I only know he made a business decision without considering the consequences. It's the same as a guy who comes into a new company and fires fifty workers to enhance his bottom line. There's not necessarily anything wrong with him enhancing his bottom line, but is there a moral problem with him firing the workers knowing they're going to have trouble getting other jobs? It's not an easy question, Brenna."

"So my dad's the bad guy in this because he's a businessman and because he made a success of the store. There's something you don't know about my dad, and you have to swear never to reveal anything I'm telling you."

If Brenna confided in him, that would mean she was starting to trust him. "I won't say a word to anyone."

She studied him keenly and he must have passed muster because she said, "My dad's father thought disciplining meant beating. He still has scars on his back from the belt."

"Brenna!"

She went on as if he hadn't interrupted. "So my dad has always tried to be a perfectionist, always tried to control everything around him, always tried to make sure that he was the one who didn't get into trouble.

Your father's restaurant was in the red. He hadn't paid his rent for six months. My dad let him go on like that, hoping the restaurant would turn around. But your father needed to make some changes to do that and he didn't want to. Dad knew he had to grow McDougall's and he did what he had to do for our family. He didn't mean to do your dad harm. He didn't do it vindictively. Behind his business decision, my dad saw the welfare of his own family. He once told us he would never let anyone control him like his father had until he was old enough to leave. He wanted to be master of his own destiny, and that's what he did. I'm sorry your dad was hurt, *and* your family, but my father isn't the bad guy here, either."

Riley just stared at Brenna and his son, wondering if motivation and intention were everything. His intention when he'd first dated her had been anything but pure. He'd wanted to take revenge on Angus McDougall by using his daughter. He felt ashamed of that now. He'd been rebellious and loyal and not very attuned to anyone's feelings but his family's. But then his affair with Brenna had turned everything on its head. If she ever found out for sure, would she understand? Why take that chance? He certainly didn't want to push her away because that would push his son away, too.

When he was quiet, she said, "I know you love your dad, Riley, and I love mine. But I have a special bond with mine. When I was four, he saved my life. We had taken a vacation to California to visit a friend of his. Their family had had a pool. I'd wandered outside one day by myself and found the gate in the fence around the pool open. Before anybody had missed me, I'd caught sight of a ball in the pool, had gone to grab it and had fallen in. I didn't know how to swim. Dad was the one who'd come rushing out. Dad was the one who'd jumped in with his clothes on, fished me out, and did mouth-to-mouth. Daddy was the one who'd ridden with me in the ambulance to the hospital to make sure I was all right."

He felt as if the wind had been knocked out of him. Recovering, he asked, "Why didn't you ever tell me any of this?"

"Because you were as angry at my dad then as your brothers still are now. I guess I thought you wouldn't believe me…that I was making it up to try to gain sympathy for him."

Derek was sleeping now at Brenna's breast, and the cover had slipped from her shoulder. Riley's gaze focused on his sleeping son and her nakedness for a few seconds, and then he lifted his gaze to hers. Her cheeks pinkened a little and he looked down again.

When she covered her breast, he wondered if she already regretted everything she'd told him. He would cherish her confidence and hoped she realized that. He didn't know what he was going to do about his brothers, but maybe his dad's suggestion of a celebration would ease the tension and promote the family atmosphere they all really wanted.

He could hope.

Riley had insisted on coming with Brenna to the pediatrician. As they walked into the doctor's office and sat in the waiting room, she had to admit she kind of liked Riley coming along. Ever since she'd learned she was pregnant, she'd been shoring up her courage to be a single mom. And she could do it. But since she'd been back in Miners Bluff, she realized how nice it was to share the responsibility.

Riley picked up a magazine and began to page

through it, but he often glanced over at Derek. Once he reached out and touched his son's cheek. Brenna's heart melted whenever he did that. Fortunately Derek slept, because their waiting time became more extended. A half hour turned into forty-five minutes and Brenna checked her watch with a worried expression.

"What's wrong?" Riley asked.

"I have a Phoenix client who was driving up for an appointment at eleven. We're not going to be out of here. I'd better give her a call."

"I can stay here with Derek," Riley offered, "If you want to go meet her."

Brenna felt torn. "I want to be here. Since he's getting a shot today, I want to be with him when he does. Let me call my client," she said. "I think she was going to visit with her sister while she's here. They were driving up together."

Brenna made the call from an alcove off the waiting room. When she returned to Riley, he looked at her with questions in his eyes.

"She wasn't happy, but I told her I knew this really good place for lunch, the Shamrock Grill, and if she and her sister wanted to have lunch there before we got together, it was on me."

Riley grinned. "You're not bad at PR."

"I've had some practice," she joked, then she remembered the conversation Riley'd had with his brother. "Are you sure you can't convince your brothers to come over for dinner some evening?"

"I'll try again, but for now I think it's a lost cause. I think we should just wait until we all get together at the restaurant next weekend. That will be easier for everyone."

She wasn't so sure about that, but she knew what

Riley meant. There would be lots of people to fill in the gaps of conversation. She wanted Derek to know his uncles as well as his aunt and his grandparents. But it was up to them what kind of relationship they'd have.

When the nurse finally motioned them back to the examination room, Brenna just wanted this visit over. The doctor came in with a smile. Dr. Rayburn had almost white hair, twinkling blue eyes and a relaxed demeanor. He shook their hands and then took Derek from Brenna. Derek wasn't too happy with having his nap disrupted. He started fussing almost immediately.

"Can I hold him while you examine him?" she asked the doctor.

"For some of the time," the doctor said. "But then I'd like to lay Derek on the table so I can check his reflexes and watch his general movement. There's more to a checkup than ears, nose and throat. I'm watching for developmental signs, too. And he needs to be able to move freely for me to see those. Okay?"

Brenna suddenly felt Riley's hand on her shoulder, and she nodded. "Okay."

The exam didn't take long and the doctor looked pleased with everything he saw.

"Weight is good," he said, checking the chart.

The nurse came in with the injection and Brenna felt herself flinch. "It will be over before you know it," the doctor told her, his voice kind.

"I can hold him now?" she asked.

"Sure, you can. This will take about two seconds." Riley squeezed her shoulder again as the doctor gave the injection and Derek cried. She felt like crying herself.

"It's all over," he said. "He shouldn't have any side effects."

"I know, I looked it up on the internet."

"A well-informed mom."

"I try to be." She'd slipped Derek back into the sling on her chest, and he was quiet now as she rocked back and forth.

Riley asked the doctor, "I don't suppose you've heard anything about the DNA test?"

Brenna stiffened. She'd forgotten all about that. She really had and she thought Riley had, too. If it was still on his mind, that meant—

She moved away from his touch on her shoulder.

The doctor said, "Be assured, my office will call you as soon as we have the results."

Brenna knew what the results would be, but apparently Riley still had doubts. The closeness she'd felt to him last night seemed to disappear in an instant. Holding Derek tightly, she avoided Riley's gaze.

Trust was always going to be an issue between them.

Chapter Nine

Riley looked like the proverbial bull in the china shop in the bridal department at McDougall's a short time later. After Brenna passed Derek to him and gave her baby a kiss, she checked around for her client. Riley had offered to drop her off and then come pick her up. So when they'd arrived, she'd gone to the back dressing room and fed Derek.

Riley glanced around at the gowns and the veils and the jewelry and the white satin shoes. He asked, "So your store looks something like this?"

"Something like this. I have a silver-and-blue theme, damask instead of cut velvet wing chairs, and more modern displays. But I do have bridal gowns all around… and lots of feminine things."

"Do any men ever come into your shop?"

She laughed. "Sure. Some women actually want their

husbands-to-be to help pick out their gown. Tradition isn't what it used to be."

"Tradition is important," Riley said. "But I guess it can change. Families are different than they used to be."

"Yes, they are."

Theirs would be if she was on the East Coast and he was here, but somehow they would be a family all the same.

A woman walked into the bridal salon in a chic pale blue suit with a sapphire necklace around her neck that Brenna knew could easily cost as much as one of her gowns.

Brenna rubbed her hand gently over Derek's head and said to Riley, "That's my client. I'll call you when I'm through."

As she moved toward Claudia Winslow, she was surprised Riley didn't leave immediately. His presence was a distraction. Riley had always been a major diversion. But she had to focus on Claudia and what she wanted.

Brenna crossed to her and shook her hand. Then she escorted her toward a Queen Anne table where she'd laid out her sketches. Claudia followed her and sat in front of the desk while Brenna sat behind it.

"I did have a great lunch at the Shamrock Grill," she admitted. "Not my usual type of restaurant, but the food was good."

"Great. I'm glad you liked it."

"So these are the sketches?"

"Yes. I'll let you study the three one by one and you can tell me what you think."

"But you will be back in New York for the fitting."

"You're planning a February wedding. We'll do the fitting some time in December. Yes, I'll be back there then."

She had to be back there. She had a business to run and a life to build for her and Derek.

Riley had been standing close enough to overhear. He gave her one last look and a nod, and then he strode out of the bridal department. Brenna had no idea what he was thinking.

An hour and a half later she still didn't know what he was thinking when he picked her up. She told him he could just pull up out front and she'd hop in the car. When she did, she noticed Derek was awake in his car seat making his little baby sounds.

Buckling in herself, she glanced at Riley as he pulled away from the department store. "What did you guys do?"

"We took a walk. I showed Derek all the changes I'd be making to the landscaping. He approved. How did it go with your client?"

"She was pleased with the designs, but when we talked about fabric and beading and stitching and what type of veil she wanted, the meeting got involved."

"Do they usually?"

"Oh, yes. Women want that bridal gown to make them feel like the most beautiful woman on earth. They want their husband-to-be's eyes to pop out of his head so he'll fall down on his knees and propose all over again."

"They put too many expectations on one day," Riley grumbled.

"Maybe. But hopes and dreams are like that, and hard to give up, no matter what the age."

"Maybe I shouldn't ask, but was this your client's first marriage? Do you even know?"

"Of course, I know. Bridal consultants are sort of like bartenders. Our clients tell us everything, and yes it is her first marriage so she wants the day to be perfect."

"Of course," he said a bit sarcastically.

She knew what Riley thought of marriage, what he'd been taught about marriage. The ironic thing was his sister and brothers had obviously not felt the same way because they *had* married. But everyone reacted differently to what happened in a family. She just wished…

What did she wish? That Riley would consider marriage? She could positively *not* be thinking that, because if she was thinking that—

She was falling for him all over again. That couldn't happen.

But as she snuck another peek at Riley, as she thought about what they'd shared as teenagers and their physical compatibility again the night of the reunion, she felt that old languorous heat creep through her.

No! She couldn't let chemistry fog her brain.

Silence pervaded the SUV during the rest of the drive and Derek was asleep by the time they reached the house. Riley carried him inside and laid him in the crib in her bedroom. The thoughts Brenna had been having in the car still nagged, so she began gathering Derek's laundry and some of her own to distract herself.

Coming into the living room, she asked Riley, "Do you need anything washed?"

He shot her an odd look. What was it about alpha males that made communication so difficult sometimes?

"I have a few T-shirts you can toss in, but you really don't have to."

"It's a load of laundry, Riley. It's no bother. I'm just being practical."

It was as if her word *practical* triggered something not so practical in Riley. He came toward her, almost like a panther stalking its prey.

"Practical? Since when are we being practical? We've

always been wildly attracted to each other, and the practical thing would have been to act on that. But our families kept us apart. Your dreams and independence kept us apart. My lack of goals and motivation kept us apart. A feud we didn't start kept us apart. The night of the reunion, we were anything but practical. So maybe, we shouldn't be so practical now."

"Riley—" She held out the flat of her hand as if she could stop him, as if she could stop herself. But he was right there in front of her, all six-foot-two of him and he was looking at her as if he wanted to gobble her up. Maybe she was looking at him the same way, but that definitely wouldn't be *practical*.

"We can't mess this up, Riley, you know that. We have to be parents."

"I don't want to mess up anything. But this heat between us is driving me crazy. Tell me you turn in at night and don't think about what it would be like if we were together in my bed. Tell me you don't think about me kissing you in places where no other man has kissed you. Tell me that climaxing in my arms isn't *exactly* what you want."

His raw honesty had her trembling, was making her knees weak, was creating pictures she'd tried to banish.

"Tell me what you want, Brenna, because I'm sure it's anything but practical."

Her voice was shaky but she stated her heart's desire anyway. "I want you to kiss me, but I'm afraid—"

He didn't let her finish. He kissed her and she forgot about everything except the passion in Riley that had always captivated her so. He'd been defiance and rebellion and hungry desire that had wrested her away from the good girl she'd been, that had wrested her away from the compliant daughter she thought she should be.

Now all of the old passion returned running headlong into new desire.

Any idea of being practical fled in the onslaught of Riley's kiss. The feel of his lips on hers, his tongue exploring her mouth, chased away any good sense she might have. His hand slid down her back and suddenly she was tight against him, feeling muscles…and his full arousal. She couldn't help but lace her fingers in his hair. When she did, his tongue thrust into her mouth deeper, demanding a fuller response.

Fire seemed to lick at her, starting in her belly, sparking in every nerve, creating such heat she believed she and Riley could go up in flames. He tasted of coffee and Riley, and she remembered how much she'd always enjoyed kissing him, *more* than enjoyed kissing him. The feel of his arms around her, the press of his body against hers made her need in a primitive way.

Riley's challenging desire suddenly changed into hungry passion. It overtook her. She forgot about breathing and thinking and only wanted to feel. The sofa wasn't very far away. Riley walked her backward as if he sensed where it was and sensed where they needed to be. They landed on it together, still in each other's arms.

Riley's kisses changed from over-the-top hungry to downright seductive. He broke away to kiss her neck, to suck her earlobe into his mouth. Before she could appreciate one sensation, there was another until his hand was under her top, until his thumb pressed across her nipple in her bra, until she knew they were going too far.

How far was too far? Too far was being in Riley's bed again. Too far was letting her emotions drown in physical passion. Too far was falling in love with him all over again.

Although it was the last thing she wanted to do, she pushed away from him. She took in a deep lungful of air, tried to order her thoughts, tried to find herself in what the two of them became when they were together. Something about Riley had always reached too far inside of her, had always led her to feel too deeply, had always led her to dream about happily-ever-after. If she let him make love to her, how would they ever find a balance again? What would they do if their families still tore them apart? What would happen to Derek?

Oh no, she didn't want to be practical. But she also didn't want her heart broken. She didn't want anything to get in the way of Riley being a father to his son. She didn't want the two of them to end up bitter and resentful and disappointed.

He took one look at her and shook his head. "Damn it, Brenna, why can't you just let go?"

"Let go? Of what? Of myself, or a life that means something to me? Of my ability to mother Derek? Of my ability to keep some perspective? No, I can't let go, Riley. There's too much at stake. Your relationship with Derek is at stake. Can't you see that?"

He ran his hand down over his face, resting his elbows on his knees, and then glanced at her out of the corner of his eye. "Dawson called while you were gone and asked if I wanted to play basketball with him and Noah and Clay. It would probably be a good idea for me to leave for a while. Are you okay with that?"

After considering a moment, realizing as he did they each needed a little space, she said, "I'm fine with that."

"If you were counting on me to help with Derek—"

"I don't want to depend on you, Riley. I'll be fine." She knew she would be. She knew she had to be.

Because when she returned to New York, she would be a single mother, and Riley would still be in Miners Bluff, a single dad.

Early that evening Riley launched a hook shot that clipped the rim of the basketball net and bounced to the ground. He didn't react on purpose. Noah, Dawson and Clay were watching him as if they expected him to erupt or to spill the beans about what was happening at his house with Brenna.

Okay, so maybe he was just being paranoid.

But when Noah joked, "Off your game tonight, O'Rourke?" and he felt like slugging the chief of police, he realized their silent scrutiny was getting to him. Maybe he should have just called Patrick and Sean and gone to the Tin Pan Tavern to have a drink with his brothers.

Dawson handed him a water bottle and Clay went after the rolling ball that was headed down Dawson's driveway. He jogged back with it and tossed it through the hoop easily. "That's how it's done," he said with a grin.

"You've got the perfect shot and the perfect life," Riley jabbed.

They all studied him.

"What?" he muttered.

"You're not yourself," Dawson said with a shake of his head. "If you tell us why you think Clay has the perfect life, maybe then we'll know what's going on with you."

Riley sighed, unscrewed the water bottle, and shook his head. "Mikala's getting to you. She's teaching you too well how to communicate."

"You make it sound like communicating isn't a good thing."

Noah's penetrating, knowing look irritated Riley even more. He took three long swallows of his water and then scowled at them all. "Do you think it's easy living under the same roof with someone you're...you're...attracted to?"

They all exchanged looks as if they weren't sure where to go from there. Clay ventured into the uncharted territory. "I imagine that could be highly frustrating."

"Damn straight, it's frustrating," Riley admitted. "The problem is, our families hate each other. Brenna and I live a country apart and neither of us want to mess up Derek's life."

"Have you talked about what you're going to do after Brenna leaves?" Noah asked with the directness of a cop.

"Some. But whenever I mention the word *custody,* she withdraws. She doesn't want to be separated from Derek and I can understand that. She wouldn't be a good mother if she did. And she *is* an excellent mother. A baby really needs to be with his mother. But that could shut me out for weeks at a time. I'll miss everything that's happening to him. Yet if I insist on joint custody and taking him say a month at a time, what will that do to *him?* What would that do to *us?*"

"Is there an 'us'?" Dawson asked.

Riley knew there was a reason why he didn't want to bring this up. He knew there was a very good reason why he should have kept his mouth shut. "I don't know if there's an 'us,'" he admitted, the water spurting out of his bottle with his hand movement.

"From the way you're acting, there's an 'us,'" Noah offered blandly.

Riley just glared at him, yet he knew Noah was right. If he didn't care, he wouldn't be this riled up.

"Brenna has a name brand and a business and a store in New York. It's not so easy to move her life," Dawson commented.

"Do you think it's easy to move mine? Clay and I are partners. I like what I do."

"What about the computer consulting work you were doing for companies that needed better web security?" Noah asked. "Couldn't you do that from anywhere?"

"I could," Riley said, thinking about it more seriously than he had before.

"You have to figure out what your priority is," Clay suggested. "If you really want to be a hands-on dad to Derek, then we'll work something out with the partnership. After all, you can open a branch in New York or Connecticut. At least you'd be closer to your son."

"IT security work would make more sense," Riley decided. "I have contacts. It wouldn't hurt to make some calls. It's not like I'd have to go ahead with anything."

"Maybe you should wait until Brenna isn't under your roof to make the decision." Noah took the ball from Clay and dribbled it a few times.

"Are you suggesting I can't make a rational decision when she's around?"

"Did you make rational decisions when she was around before?" Clay asked.

These guys were getting too good at noticing and remembering. "Cease and desist," he said with a resigned sigh. "I don't want Brenna to know I'm even thinking about this. Not a word to anybody, not even your wives. You know how women talk."

"*We're* talking," Dawson pointed out.

"Maybe you should try communicating with Brenna," Noah concluded.

He'd like to communicate with her, all right, he thought. But his idea of communication and what Noah was suggesting were probably very different.

The next day Brenna hurried toward the Shamrock Grill pleased with the work she'd accomplished that morning. The gowns had been delivered from her store in New York to McDougall's bridal salon. The models for the runway part of the extravaganza had stopped in for their fittings. She and Katie had gone over the flower arrangements, spoken with the managers of the other departments and made headway with all the preparations. Riley had known her mom would be babysitting for her today and he'd left a note this morning before he'd taken tourists on an excursion of the area. It had read that if she could get away, she should meet him at the Shamrock Grill at two. He'd signed it *R*.

When they'd been dating in high school, he'd often passed her notes like that—where they would meet and when—and signed them the same way. He'd never signed them *Love, Riley.* He'd never used the word. Maybe that's another reason why she hadn't felt…secure with his feelings for her. He wasn't telling her what he felt now, either. Oh yeah, he desired her. But was there more underneath the passion? Would she ever know?

As she entered the Shamrock Grill, the scents of onion, baked meat loaf and simmering stew welcomed her. It was old world and rustic and always full of good smells. Liam was at one of the tables, talking to customers.

When he saw her, however, he excused himself and came toward her with a smile. "I'm glad you could come.

Riley's out back. I told him I'd keep an eye out for you. He wasn't too sure you'd make it, though."

She wasn't exactly sure what to say to that. It sounded as if Liam was fishing for something but she wasn't sure what. "The day worked out like it was supposed to for a change. I finished with everything at the store, and Mom has Derek, so—"

She suddenly realized how that all sounded—like she was still committed to her family, first and foremost. And she was, wasn't she? Derek was part of that now, and she still wasn't sure how Riley fit in.

After a quick frown, Liam shrugged. "Well, I'm glad it worked out. There are tables under umbrellas in the back. I open that section in the spring and fall. Riley thought you might like to eat out there. Come on, I'll show you to a table."

Liam led her out back to a set of tables with green-and-white-striped umbrellas. There were a few potted plants around, too, with pink and purple petunias and ivy vines. The tables were empty except for one where Riley sat. He cracked a smile when he saw her, but she wasn't sure it was a real one. His real smiles were for Derek, not for her. When he looked at her, he just looked puzzled, as if he didn't know what to do about her, or the situation or the desire he felt.

"I thought if we let the lunch crowd thin out, we'd have some privacy," Riley said, giving his dad a pointed look.

"You do want lunch, don't you?" Liam asked with an arched brow. "Or would you like to go to the kitchen and get it yourself?"

Riley looked a bit chagrinned. "I didn't mean it that way. I just meant it would be great if you don't have to seat someone else out here."

"Got it," Liam said with a nod. "And I'll send my most discreet waitress so we don't start any gossip."

"There's already gossip," Riley said with a frown.

"I won't ask any questions," Liam assured them. "Just let me know if you need anything besides the waitress."

Liam glanced at Brenna, ignoring his son's comment. "Say goodbye before you leave."

Brenna smiled. "I will."

Sitting here with Riley felt odd. After all, this wasn't a date. Had she been hoping it was? No, of course not. But she had been hoping Riley wanted some time alone. But now she suspected that wasn't the case. He had something on his mind.

"What gossip have you heard?" she asked as casually as she could since that seemed to be on his mind. Since she'd be going back to New York, she really wasn't concerned about her reputation. But her parents lived here as well as his family, and *he* was the one who would have to field questions when she left.

"I stopped at the Rocky D after the tour to check how many horses would be available tomorrow when I take a group to Feather Peak."

She remembered the last time he'd gone to Feather Peak, and from the look in his eyes, so did he. She waited.

"Tim Levinson boards his horse at the Rocky D."

"I remember Tim."

Riley's eyes narrowed. "He asked you out before you and I were...involved."

Brenna smiled, remembering. "Yes, he did. We had a great time. His father had lent him his convertible and we drove around, just letting the wind make us feel... free. Tim wasn't at the reunion, I don't think."

"No, he wasn't. Zack said he'd gotten tied up on business in Phoenix. He has an electronics store in Flagstaff now."

"So what does Tim have to do with gossip?"

"He heard you were back in town. He heard you'd had a baby and you were staying with me. He was pumping Zack to find out if you were here to stay, if anything was going on between the two of us, because apparently he wants to ask you out again."

Brenna didn't know what to say to that, so she simply said, "He does?"

"Yeah, and I just wondered what you'd say if he asked you."

Her gaze shot to Riley's. "And you would or wouldn't approve if I went on a date with him?"

"You're living under my roof."

"And that means—"

From what she could tell, Riley didn't lose his temper any more, not since he'd learned self-discipline in the Marines. At least that's the impression he gave.

But right now he looked as if it was about to blow. "I don't know what the hell it means. That's the problem."

"The bridal fashion show is in a week. After that I'll help Dad tie up some odds and ends. But then I'm returning to New York. Dating anyone is the last thing on my mind. If Tim would want to have lunch for old times' sake, sure I'd go to lunch with him if I can fit it in. But that's all it would be, Riley, a lunch. I don't even know how I'm going to handle working and raising Derek. I don't need some kind of romantic entanglement thrown into the mix."

Riley's eyes narrowed as he studied her, as if he was trying to see the real truth. "You seem to be handling work and Derek just fine now."

"But that's because you're around to help, too, and I

know my mom will babysit whenever I need her. Back in New York, I'm going to have to depend on my sitter."

"Have you given *any* consideration to joint custody?"

She sighed. "Is that really what this lunch is about? You want to convince me that handing over Derek to you six months of the year would be the best thing for him and for us?"

"I didn't ask you here just to talk about gossip or joint custody." He blew out a breath. "We never get any time alone and I thought we needed some." He leaned forward and caressed her face.

The sensation of his thumb on her cheek ran through her, heating up the spring day, making her feel as if the sun was shining on her even though they were sitting in the shade of the umbrella. Did he really care? Or was he just trying to get his way?

"Zack and Jenny are having a barbecue at the Rocky D on Sunday," he said. "Would you like to go?"

This time she needed to have something perfectly clear. "Is it a date?"

"It could be, if we want to think about it that way."

Heaven help her, she *did* want to think about it that way. "A barbecue sounds like fun. We could use a little fun. I can ask Mom to watch Derek."

"Sounds good," Riley said, looking at her as if he wanted to kiss her, right then and there.

Suddenly a waitress came out the back door of the restaurant and approached their table. Riley looked unhappy, but Brenna felt relieved. If she and Riley did kiss in public, they'd be making a statement. She didn't know if she was ready to make any kind of statement with him. Yes, she was falling for him again. That scared her down to her pink toenail polish.

Chapter Ten

A barbecue at the Rocky D had the same spirited enthusiasm as a county fair, Brenna decided as she and Riley parked near the barns. The spacious rear veranda was decorated with colorful lanterns and pots of pink geraniums. Tall speakers were positioned at either end and she imagined there might be dancing there later. Right now everyone was milling about under yellow canopies where picnic tables and benches were lined up family style.

"Zack's dad sure knows how to throw a party," Riley remarked as they passed the beautiful rose garden with its tiered fountain in the middle. They walked side by side as they headed into the aromas that rode the air—barbecued ribs, sizzling beef, roasting chicken as well as the underlying scent of pine and sage.

Brenna had worn red jeans with a white tank trimmed in red. Her platform sandals along with the gold chain around her neck dressed up the outfit. She waved at Mikala who was seated at one of the tables with Dawson and his son Luke. Clay and Celeste were seated there, too, with their daughter Abby. Zack was talking to one of the waiters at the long buffet table and he waved when he saw them.

"You and Zack were friends back in high school, weren't you?" Riley asked.

"I didn't run around in the same crowd, but I came to the Rocky D to ride. He knew I liked to paint and draw, and one year he gave me a picture of his mom's favorite horse and asked me to paint a Christmas ornament that he could give to her. But he never had eyes for anybody other than Jenny, if that's what you're asking me."

"I knew he was always sweet on Jenny. But they didn't really hook up until she did an internship with his mom here at the Rocky D their senior year in high school. The Deckers gave her the first real home she'd known. Her dad came to her wedding, though, and I heard he's visited a couple of times since."

They watched as Silas Decker exited the back door of the house and headed for Zack. When he reached him, he put his hand on his son's shoulder.

"Zack and his dad have found common ground, after all these years," Riley added. "It's a good thing to see."

Brenna would have started forward to mingle, but Riley caught her elbow. "You said you used to paint. I don't remember that from high school."

"I had a small studio set up at home. I spent a lot of time there when I was feeling confused, or needed a break from the rest of the world."

"Do you still paint?"

"I don't have time. Once I entered design school, I spent all of my hours designing."

"But if it's something you like to do, you shouldn't let it go."

"Maybe when Derek's older, maybe when I have enough help, maybe..." She stopped. "Maybe when we have forty-eight hour days."

"You can't work and take care of Derek all the time. You need something for *you*, too."

"And what do *you* have?" she asked, intrigued by this side of Riley.

"I like to ride up to Horsethief Canyon and camp out, or do Sudoku."

She laughed. "You're kidding."

"No, I'm not. It's my guilty pleasure." The way he was looking at her made her think about all kinds of guilty pleasures she'd like to experience with him.

He was dressed in a chambray snap-buttoned shirt with jeans and a good pair of boots. With his casually cut black hair and his very blue eyes she thought he was the sexiest man alive. But she couldn't tell him that, of course, at least not here, and not now.

The way he was looking at her made her say, "Let's mingle."

Within a few minutes Brenna and Riley separated. Brenna drifted into a catch-up conversation with Jenny and then Katie joined them. It felt good to be reconnecting with women she once knew. Riley drifted over to Zack and Silas where Noah joined in. But Brenna's gaze was never far from Riley's and she caught him watching her, too. It was an odd feeling, coming to the barbecue together yet not really being a couple.

Did she *want* to be part of a couple? Ever since she'd found Thad with her roommate, she hadn't felt she'd ever want to be part of a couple again. A romantic relationship always seemed to cause heartache. Leaving Riley all those years ago had hurt. Thad leaving her had hurt. Maybe she'd considered that pain as payback. Maybe she'd thought she'd deserved it. But if she'd stayed in Miners Bluff after graduation, and she and Riley had gone public, what would have happened to them? Neither of them had been mature enough to handle a serious relationship. And now there were no easy answers.

When Silas' housekeeper Martha beckoned Jenny to come into the kitchen, Katie said to Brenna, "You seem a hundred miles away."

"Only a hundred?" Brenna joked.

"Are you worrying about your business in New York? I can't imagine running it long distance. Staying on top of everything in the flower shop is difficult enough while I'm here."

"No, I'm not worried about New York. I mean, yes, I have to get back, but I check in every day. We videoconference and my sales force keeps me apprised of everything that's going on."

"So it's Riley?" Katie asked.

She and Katie had gotten closer over the past week and Brenna had noticed something about Katie, too, that she wanted to ask her friend about. But first she said, "Yes, it's Riley. How do you know when something old is new? And how do you know when something's new that it won't break your heart all over again?"

"I know what you mean," Katie assured her, and that gave Brenna an opening.

"You seemed to be avoiding Noah earlier. When he steps into a group, you leave it. Weren't you friends in high school?"

Looking a bit flustered for a moment, Katie finally responded, "Noah and Ross were best friends."

Katie's husband had been dead for over two years

now, but that didn't mean her grief had diminished. "I'm sorry. I shouldn't have brought it up."

"No, it's okay. I guess you're right. I have been avoiding Noah. But that's hard to do when we have the same friends, and are sometimes invited to the same parties. I like Noah. He's a great guy. But I—" She looked away for a few moments up to Moonshadow Mountain. "I guess I just feel awkward with him because sometimes I don't want to talk about Ross. It's hard to explain."

"If you ever want to talk about it, I'm just a phone call away."

"Thank you. Returning to Miners Bluff hasn't been easy. My parents loved Ross so, and I talk about him with them. It's just that sometimes it's…hard."

Brenna was trying to find something comforting to say when she felt a gentle hand on her shoulder. "Brenna, dear, it's so good to see you again."

Brenna turned toward the comforting voice and knew who it was immediately. "Ms. Conti! Hello. It's been a long time."

"Too long. You're even more beautiful now than you were in high school. Hi there, Katie. It's good to see you, too. The way you've redone the flower shop is fabulous."

"And we appreciate your orders," Katie said easily with a smile. Possibly sensing Anna Conti wanted to speak with Brenna, she said, "If you'll excuse me, I'm going to circulate a bit."

After "see you laters" Brenna remarked, "So you're still running the Purple Pansy."

"I certainly am. But I'm not sure how much longer—"

Suddenly there was a loud tapping against a handheld microphone and a deep male voice asked, "Can I have your attention, please?"

Everyone turned toward the veranda where Silas was standing. His gaze met Anna's and he motioned to her.

Anna leaned close to Brenna. "I think it's time to reveal a little secret. You'll soon find out why. I want to speak to you again later." Then Anna was off to the veranda to join Silas. Zack's father didn't hesitate to put his arm around her.

He said, "We've invited you all here today for a barbecue, that's true. But we also had an ulterior motive. We've kept a lid on this for the past week, and only Zack and Jenny, Mikala and Dawson knew. But Anna and I would like all of you to share in our happiness as we announce our engagement. Miss Conti has done me the honor of agreeing to marry me!"

Sudden applause burst from all around Brenna and she started applauding, too. She watched as Jenny, Zack, Mikala, Dawson and Luke joined Silas and Anna on the veranda, all of them looking overjoyed.

"Let's see the ring," one of Silas's friends called out.

He laughed, took something from the pocket of his jeans and slipped it onto Anna's finger. She held it up for all to see.

Brenna caught a glimpse of a wonderfully huge solitaire wrapped in a circle of rubies. It suited Anna perfectly.

The Deckers' guests crowded all around to congratulate the couple and Brenna joined the makeshift receiving line. She sensed Riley's approach before she saw him, but then he was beside her looking very surprised.

"Did you know about this?" she asked him.

"Silas and Aunt Anna have been dating since last Thanksgiving, but no, I didn't see this coming. I wonder what she'll do with the Purple Pansy."

"Any chance Mikala would run it?"

"I doubt it. She'll be tied up with a baby soon. With a new marriage, becoming a mother to Luke and keeping up with her practice, I'm not sure she'll want to take that on. Since Mikala married, I think Aunt Anna has hired someone to help her, but I don't know if she'll be capable of running the place for her."

Brenna realized how much she wanted some things to stay the same. "The Purple Pansy has been part of Miners Bluff for decades. I hate to think of it not being open."

"I know, but Aunt Anna has to do what's best for her now." Brenna supposed that was a decision everyone had to make at some point.

After the announcement, Anna waved to Brenna. She apparently had something very important on her mind. Together Brenna and Riley approached the patio and Brenna hugged Anna. "I'm so happy for you."

"I'm happy for me, too! That's what I wanted to talk to you about. Will you design a gown for me?"

"Of course I will."

"Spare no expense," Silas added, gazing at Anna with so much love, Brenna felt her eyes growing misty.

"I know you need plenty of notice," Anna added. "We're thinking of getting married around Christmas. Is six months enough?"

"I'll make it enough. Why don't I give you a call next week and we can get together."

"That sounds wonderful. And just to give you an idea, I want it in pale pink with a little bit of lace and a few pearls. It can even be a little old-fashioned, or a little bit Western. Let your imagination run wild."

Brenna laughed. "I'll do that. Just your description makes me want to start sketching."

Silas gave Riley and Brenna a considering look.

"Now I think its time for a little fun. Jenny's going to put on some music and I want to see the two of you out there on the dance floor…well, dance patio…tonight."

Brenna wasn't sure what to say. What if Riley didn't want to dance?

Just then music blared through the speakers, a ballad made for romance. Silas gave a little bow to Anna and then offered her his hand.

Brenna didn't turn toward Riley…didn't meet his gaze. She could take off and mingle if he wanted nothing to do with the dancing on the patio.

But then she felt his hand on her shoulder. "Could I have this dance?"

She automatically filled in the rest of the line from the country ballad. "For the rest of my life." She scolded herself for even thinking it.

This is a barbecue. You're just being social. Having Riley's arm around you is the way people dance. That common sense advice didn't keep her heart from pounding so loud that she could hardly hear herself think.

She let him lead her to a corner of the patio where, once in his arms, they moved in time with the music. Neither of them said anything for several beats, then Riley asked, "Is six months pushing it for a custom-made gown?"

Brenna thought about the process. "I'll make it a priority."

"Silas won't quibble on the price. This could be one of the most expensive gowns you've ever made."

"No, it won't, because I'm not going to charge her."

Riley stopped and stared at her with a puzzled expression. "You're kidding."

"No, I'm not. Aunt Anna has always been like a favorite aunt. I didn't hang around her as much as Jenny and Celeste and Mikala did, but there were a few times when she was just there when I needed her."

"Like?"

"Like when I was dating you, and didn't know if I should be or not."

"You told her about us?"

"Not exactly. Aunt Anna has this gift of seeing more than we give her credit for. I don't know if you remember, but one day after school, you picked me up in back of the library. She was coming around the corner and she saw us. I ran into her in the department store about a week later. I was worried she'd tell my family. She was always so honest about everything. Taking me aside, she just mentioned she saw me with you, and that was my business. Then she added that I should follow my heart, no matter what anybody else thought."

Riley looked troubled for a moment as if he wanted to ask her something. Yet he didn't. She had followed her heart that year, but maybe she hadn't followed it far enough.

She thought about their son and Riley's place in Derek's life. Her mom was babysitting tonight. When she'd arrived at Riley's house, he'd been warmer to her than previously. So Brenna said, "Thanks for being friendlier to my mom tonight. She appreciated it. I could tell."

"She's good with Derek. And I…well…" He hesitated then said with the determination she knew so well, "Things have to change. I had a phone call with Dad this afternoon. He's going to invite your parents to the restaurant for our celebration next weekend. So maybe you can soften up your dad and encourage him to come."

"And you think he'll listen to me?"

"I think you have influence. I also think he'll do anything *you* want him to do if he has the right motivation."

"You want me to use his grandson to get him there?"

"I just think if we all put Derek first, our families will have something to build on."

Could today be a milestone? As they danced Riley eased her closer to him. His pressure was subtle on her back. His hand held hers a little tighter as he brought it into his chest. The music drifted around them, and Brenna knew in his arms was where she wanted to be. Darkness had begun to fall and the shadows were thick at the edge of the patio. That's where they stayed as one dance segued into the next, as Brenna's pulse raced, as she felt Riley become aroused, as neither of them moved away.

As she felt his lips at her temple, she became afraid… afraid to love and lose, but more afraid to not even love at all.

It was almost eleven when Brenna settled Derek in his crib. After she and Riley had returned from the barbecue, he'd insisted on following her mom home to make sure she arrived safely. Brenna was grateful for that and grateful his attitude seemed to be changing.

She still wasn't used to the night silence after living so many years in New York. The barbecue at the Deckers had brought back memories of the days she'd gone riding there, of her senior year with Riley. When they'd danced together tonight—

She put the thoughts aside. Instead she considered Anna's wedding gown. Maybe she'd sketch tonight if she couldn't sleep. Thinking about style and adornment and material, she decided to get ready for bed.

She shut her door as she normally did at night, then undressed. She was in her bra and panties when a design idea came to her that just couldn't wait. Picking up her sketchbook on the dresser, she flipped to a blank page and began drawing before she forgot the lines, the neck, the length of the sleeves. This was the way creativity happened sometimes.

She was so engrossed in what she was doing that she wasn't aware that Riley had come home until there was a quick rap on her door and then it opened. Riley had done the same thing many times before. She usually took her robe to the bathroom with her, showered and undressed and wrapped herself in that. She'd taken care never to be naked when he was around. But tonight, well—

When the door opened and he stepped inside, fully expecting her to still be clothed, she froze and so did he. He didn't say he was sorry. He didn't close the door and leave. Rather he stepped inside and just stood there, canvassing her body as if he'd never seen it before.

"What are you doing?" he asked, as if they were going to have a conversation with her in her bra and panties and him fully clothed.

"Riley—" She supposed his name was a warning. She supposed she should grab her robe and cover herself.

"Is that your uniform for working late at night?" he joked, his voice husky.

"Riley," she said again in exasperation, setting her sketchbook on the dresser, setting her pencil beside it. She should cover herself, she really should. She should feel awkward and self-conscious. She really should.

But she didn't, and the way his blue eyes were darkening, she felt flattered.

He nodded to the lacy pink bra and high-cut panties she was wearing. "Is that what you wore tonight?"

"Yes."

"If you had told me that, or shown me before we left, I never would have gotten through the night."

Her mouth went dry. But somehow she managed to ask, "What would you have done?"

"I would have dragged you into one of the stalls in the barn and made love to you. And don't say my name again as if you want to prevent what's going to happen next."

She couldn't let this happen. She had to make a dash for that robe. The problem was, she'd have to slide around him to get it.

With a quick decision, she made a valiant try. But it wasn't quite valiant enough. He didn't let her slip past him. He wrapped his arm around her and brought her up close.

"Maybe we should dance with you dressed like this." His voice was low and as seductive as all get out. He moved with her as if they might have been dancing to music of their own, music only they could hear. She gave in to the sway of his thighs against hers until she felt his hand at her back unhook her bra. Before she could say his name again, he kissed her.

Tonight she followed Riley where he was trying to lead her. Maybe it had been their conversation after they'd arrived at the barbecue. Maybe it had been their sensual dance there. Maybe it had been his care in making sure her mom got home okay. Maybe it was just Riley himself. She couldn't resist this pull toward him any longer. He'd always been irresistible to her, so she might as well stop denying it.

When he scooped her up to carry her to his bedroom, she began unfastening the snaps on his shirt.

"You have too many clothes on," she murmured right before she kissed his neck.

"I'm going to remedy that really fast," he muttered, walking quickly to the bed and laying her on his mattress. He stared down at her and asked, "You aren't going to change your mind, are you?"

"No," she said, meaning it. Even if they only had tonight, she wanted it. She wanted *him*.

He didn't bother turning on the light. The glow from the hall barely reached inside the room. She heard the rustle of fabric and she imagined he was taking off his shirt. There was silence until his belt clanked against the wooden chair. When she heard the rasp of the zipper, she became even more excited than she already was.

She slipped her bra from her shoulders, letting it drop to the floor. She felt his weight on the bed, heard a drawer open and close, then knew he was barely a foot away. When she turned toward him, he reached for her, tipped her chin up, then kissed her long and hard and deep.

After that Riley didn't give her time to breathe. His tongue darted between her lips hungrily. She accepted his hunger and returned it with her own. There was fierceness about his passion tonight, as if he needed to convince her of something. Convince her they were good together in bed? Convince her they could be good parents? Convince her to stay?

Each kiss carried more heat. Each touch brought their intimacy to a new level. She filled her hands with him, ran them over his back as he held on and so did she. She didn't even realize she was still wearing her panties until he kissed first one breast then the other, heading toward her navel. Her lingerie was a guilty pleasure and these pink filmy dress bikinis were one of her favorite pair. But they soon became a means of torture as Riley rimmed his thumb around the material at her leg, as his teeth nipped at the fabric right below her navel, as his fingers pressed through the pink froth right where she needed his touch most.

"Riley," she cried.

He stopped what he was doing. "Do you want to leave them on, or do you want to take them off?"

"Off," she said, breathlessly, and he chuckled. It was such a deep, sexy chuckle.

After he skimmed the fabric down her legs and she kicked them off, he came back to her again but not to her lips. His lips moved to her navel. She and Riley had shared intimacy before, but it had been pretty traditional. Now he was doing something he'd never done before, something she had no control over, something that made her feel so vulnerable. He kissed his way to her most intimate place, nibbled, licked, touched and brought her to such a frenzied arousal she thought she'd come apart. She grabbed at his shoulders, needing so much from him…needing things she couldn't name. But he didn't move, he didn't raise his head, he just kept revving up the sensations until an orgasm rocked her so hard, she could hardly gasp air into her lungs.

But he didn't give her any time to absorb what had happened. He prepared himself, rose above her, and said, "We're not finished yet."

She opened her arms and raised her legs to accept him fully. He pressed into her quickly while sensations still tingled throughout her body, as if he'd planned it that way. They rocked together, their groans and moans building in a crescendo as their skin glistened with their desire, as their need became all encompassing, as Riley sought his release but only if he took her with him again.

So many primitive sensations barraged Brenna. She felt as if she were involved in an elemental mating she'd never known before. Before, they'd both kept their guard up. Before, their families were walls that couldn't be beaten down. Before, they hadn't had a son who meant the world to both of them. Something beyond them now bound them together. Something beyond them transformed this into lovemaking they'd never experienced before. She couldn't stop stroking his hair, raking her nails down his back, arching into him to give him more. She wanted to give him her love. So much love. But could he accept her love? Could he accept her? Could he accept change?

Passion burned away the smoky questions and doubts and took them to a new meeting of bodies…maybe even souls. When Brenna's second orgasm began, she accepted each of Riley's thrusts, eager for his climax, too. It happened simultaneously, shaking them and the bed and their whole world.

Afterward they lay there, stunned, without breath, exhausted and spent. Brenna knew Riley would want to talk about it, but she didn't. She just wanted to hold on to the moment and hold on to him.

He rolled to his side and asked, "How do you feel?"

She wanted to say, *So in love with you I could cry,* but she didn't. "I feel good, how about you?"

"The best. *You're* the best, Brenna. You always were."

She could take that so many ways, and maybe she did need to talk about what had happened, too. "Why am I the best, Riley?"

"Because you respond and you react and you go with your passion."

That wasn't exactly what she'd expected to hear. Another question might clarify more, but—

Riley wrapped his arms around her and pulled her against him. They both turned, facing the same direction and she nestled in his arms. He kissed her behind her ear lobe and with that kiss, she knew he was telling her that he cared.

But just how *much?*

Chapter Eleven

Every time Riley stepped into McDougall's Department Store he cringed. But he knew he had to get over it. His son could inherit this someday. That was the strangest thought he'd had yet, and he'd had a lot of them the past week, as Brenna had shared his bed. They'd always had great physical chemistry, but now… Something more shook him up whenever they had sex. Maybe it was just that Derek was across the hall. This morning Riley had gotten the call that confirmed his paternity. Brenna didn't even know the results yet. Then again, that was stupid thinking, because she'd known the results all along and he should have known them, too.

Had he really had any doubt? Or had the mistrust he'd felt about women all his life convinced him to go through with that DNA test? The rustle and noise of customers taking advantage of McDougall's wedding extravaganza's sales bombarded Riley as he moved deeper into the store. He had two reasons to be here. The first, to tell Brenna about the DNA results and to also tell her he was sorry for asking for the test. And the second—he was just curious about this production and how she'd been a part of it. He wanted to see the end result.

He saw how different the store looked right away. A huge, flower-covered arch with a sign on top announced, *Bridal Extravaganza—Storewide.*

The extent of the theme was easy to see with tulle and glitter and boxes wrapped in silver and gold standing on counters and on displays. Silvery wedding bells hung from the ceiling. The shoe department had a huge display of brides' and bridesmaids' shoes. A beautiful doll in a white gown front and center on the perfume counter stood next to what he assumed was one of the most expensive bottles of perfume in the store and a tall fresh flower arrangement. As he stepped under the arch and walked down the main aisle, he spotted customers lining up in rows around the stairway. The bridal show was at 11:00 a.m. and he should be just in time for it. If he could merely pull Brenna aside for a few minutes—

He ran up the stairs, two at a time, and immediately noticed another hub of activity. Models in bridal gowns seemed to be everywhere with veils flowing and trains trailing and a scent of flowers strong from all the bouquets. He caught sight of Brenna on her knees, needle and thread in hand, doing something to one of the model's trains. Her peach-colored pantsuit brought out the creaminess of her skin, the expressiveness of her eyes, the glossiness of her blond hair that she'd wound up in a tight mound at the back of her head. A few tendrils danced around her face and he wanted to twirl them in his fingers and take down her hair. As he studied her, his fantasies began to play because he knew about the peach undergarments she wore beneath that pantsuit. He'd told her he'd drop Derek off at his sister's and then he'd try to catch the show.

So here he was, and here she was, and when their gazes met all he wanted to do was grin. She held up her hand to him as if to say, Just a minute. Then she trimmed a thread, told the model she was good to go and rose to her feet.

When she approached him, her cheeks were flushed and she looked a bit harried. "We're about ready to start. The makeup consultant is finishing a few of the girls in the back."

"Can I steal you for a minute? I promise, only a minute."

She glanced around and seemed to be satisfied with what she saw. She motioned for him to follow her and they stepped behind one of the huge placards announcing the extravaganza. "Is everything okay?"

"Everything's fine. Derek's with Shannon and Jakie's treating him like he's a crown prince."

She laughed. "I don't know if that's good or bad."

He got to the point. "I got a phone call this morning from the doctor's office. The DNA results came in. You already know what the probability of me being Derek's dad is."

"Yes, I do," she said somberly.

"I'm sorry I pushed for the test."

Her eyes widened. "You wanted to be sure."

"I should have been sure without the test. I just wanted you to know that."

Her expression became so beautiful he wanted to carry her away. "Thank you for saying it."

He took a step closer to her, couldn't help but taking her chin in his palm and kissing her.

Suddenly there was a loud clearing of the throat.

Riley ended the kiss and stepped back. When he peered around the sign he saw Angus McDougall, who didn't look any too happy. "So this has been going on the whole time you two have been under the same roof?"

"Daddy," Brenna started, "this isn't the place to talk about—"

"No, I agree. It isn't. Maurice says he needs you in the back."

Brenna looked from Riley to her father, obviously not wanting to leave them alone together.

But Riley just said, "It's okay. Go on. I'll be downstairs watching with everyone else in a few minutes."

After a last worried look at the two of them, Brenna went to find Maurice.

Riley said, "I'd better get downstairs. I don't want to miss any of this."

But Angus wasn't going to let him walk away that easily. "What are you planning to do after Brenna leaves?"

"Do about what?" Riley asked.

"I assume you'll want to spend time with your son."

"Yes, I will."

"You realize a child needs his mother."

"A child needs both of his parents."

"Brenna intends to stay in New York."

"I know that. But there are cross-country flights and I intend to make use of them."

"You and Brenna are in agreement about how you're going to handle this?" Angus's question was as clipped as the rest of the conversation.

Riley wasn't about to tell Brenna's dad that they didn't have an agreement about anything yet, so he simply said, "We'll do what's best for Derek."

Angus studied him as if analyzing the truth of the words. "I hope so. My wife called your father yesterday. We'll be attending the party at the Shamrock tomorrow evening."

Riley felt relieved. "Good. I'm glad you and your wife can make it. That's important to Brenna."

"Yes, I know. And we would do anything for Brenna."

Riley realized if he stood here with Angus McDougall much longer they just might get into an argument. He said again, "I'd better get downstairs."

This time Angus didn't argue with him.

Brenna knew she was smiling wider than she ever had. She felt like singing. She felt like shouting from Moonshadow Mountain that Riley trusted her. She'd seen it in his eyes. She really had. She hadn't rushed to Maurice right away. Instead she'd watched her father and Riley while they were talking. They hadn't been smiling. But they hadn't looked as if they were at each other's throats, either. Just maybe…

Just maybe what? She and Riley would end up together? When he didn't believe in marriage? Did getting married really matter? To her it did. She realized that as she watched the models in their wedding gowns one by one, descend the stairs. Today she understood that vows for a lifetime meant so much more than having sex, having an affair, living together.

Was she as traditional as her parents? Maybe she was. After all, how could she design bridal gowns without believing in what they symbolized?

As the last model made her way down the grand staircase, Brenna followed, ready to talk to her father's customers, to explain the design process, to speak about what that special day would mean. Simply put, this whole bridal extravaganza was about starting a life together, having friends and family contribute to a couple's wish list. That wish list wasn't just about things. It was about having a life together and believing in tomorrow.

Midway down the stairs she spotted Riley, who was gazing up at her. She'd returned to Miners Bluff hoping Riley would want to be a dad, hoping somehow they could parent together. But now she wanted so much more.

When she reached the first floor, Riley crossed to her and then gestured to all of the models who were circulating and the customers buzzing around them. "You've created a real event for your dad."

"Maybe more than he bargained for," she admitted with a smile.

"You mean when he asked you to help he didn't realize you were a force to be reckoned with?"

"Something like that."

A woman near the jewelry counter waved to Brenna and Brenna held up a finger to tell her she'd just be a minute. She wanted to stand here with Riley, hear everything he had to say and just be with him. But doggone it, she still didn't want to let her father down. She wanted this day to be a huge success.

"I know you have to go," he said, understanding. "But when I dropped Derek off at Shannon's, I asked her if she'd mind watching him through this evening, too. What time do you think you'll be done here?"

"The store closes at 6:00. I should be home by 7:00, 7:30." Home. She was beginning to think of his place that way.

"How about if I pick up something for dinner and we

eat out on the patio? It's going to be a beautiful night. I thought we'd have some…alone time that way."

She could see in his eyes exactly what that alone time would consist of, and she liked the idea. She liked it a whole lot. "That sounds great. Do you want me to call you when I'm on the way?"

"That would be good. I'm going to be at Clay's this afternoon going over schedules and gear, seeing who's going to take what tours next week. If you need me, just call my cell."

He reached out, took her hand and gave it a squeeze. She squeezed his back. She *would* call if she needed him. She'd started to depend on him. That meant *she* trusted *him,* too. Tonight maybe they'd talk about where they went from here.

Four hours later Riley dumped the ribs into the slow cooker as his father had suggested, adding extra sauce. After he took his shower, he'd slide the pan of potatoes au gratin into the oven. He'd already divided the Caesar salad from the Shamrock into two dishes and covered them with plastic wrap. He'd wrapped the cornbread muffins with aluminum foil and he'd pop them in the oven as soon as Brenna called. All of the glitter at the bridal sale had sparked another idea, too, and he'd even stopped at one of the touristy gift shops to buy candles. He'd have time to ready the patio after his shower.

Suddenly there was a loud knock on his door. He was puzzled as to who his visitor might be until the door opened and Patrick walked in.

"Hey, Bro," Patrick said.

"Patrick. What are you doing here?"

"You don't want to see me?"

"Sure, I do. But you said you wouldn't come over as long as Brenna was here."

"She's not here," Patrick responded with a grin. "I stopped at Shannon's. She said Brenna would be tied up at her daddy's store all day."

"So you met Derek?" Riley asked, trying to keep the conversation casual and away from a hot topic.

"Fine son you've got there. Are you sure yet that he's yours?"

When Patrick learned his wife had been unfaithful, he'd been hurt so deeply he couldn't seem to recover. What had happened still clouded his judgment. "We got the DNA results back. I'm definitely Derek's father."

"Then what are you going to do about it?"

Riley could tell from Patrick's tone that his brother was ready for an argument. *He* wasn't. He'd learned a lot of things in the marines, and how to diffuse a potential blowup was one of them. "Would you like a beer?"

"Sure. I've got time."

"You're not seeing the kids this weekend?" Timmy was four and Brad was six, and Patrick saw them as much as his ex-wife would let him.

"Nope. Next weekend is my weekend. And that's what I wanted to talk to you about."

Uh-oh. Riley had stepped into that one. He went to the refrigerator and took out two beers. After he popped the caps, he handed one to his brother. "So this isn't just a visit? You had a reason for stopping by?"

"This was a rare chance I had to talk to you without Brenna being around." He took a card from his pocket and laid it on the counter. "That's the name of a lawyer who handles custody agreements. He's good. I used him."

Riley shook his head. "Brenna and I are going to work this out."

"Oh, really? After she's back in New York, how easy will it be to reach her? You need to settle this before she leaves. You need your rights in writing."

Did he? Or could he trust that Brenna would do the right thing and let him see Derek as often as they both thought was necessary? He remembered what Angus had said about a child needing its mother. He remembered when his mother had left and the gaping hole in his life. He wasn't sure that having rights on paper would do anything more than divide him and Brenna.

Yet knowing Patrick was like a dog with a bone when he got something into his head, Riley said, "I'll think about it."

As if Patrick guessed that was all he was going to get for now, he nodded, took a swig of his beer and then asked, "So who do you think is going to win the game tonight?"

Brenna walked in the door of Riley's house and all was quiet. She laid her briefcase and purse on the sofa, then went to find him, excitement making her pulse race a little faster. He was on the patio and she stopped in her tracks when she saw him.

The cedar table had two place settings with napkins folded beside the silverware. A water glass and a wine glass sat at the tip of each knife. There was a bouquet of white daisies in the center of the table and a candle in a hurricane globe lit beside it. Flameless candles decorated a side table, and two were perched on the brick wall. Riley had laid kindling in the outdoor fireplace and she expected he'd light it as night moved in.

With one glance she could tell he'd gone to a lot of trouble.

"What's all this?" She approached him slowly, not knowing exactly how to act. She'd spent time in his bed, on and off, since they'd made love last weekend. But this?

This was special.

"This," he said with a slow smile, "is an official date. This…is just for us without any distractions." He picked up a gift bag on one of the chairs. "I thought you might like to change into something comfortable."

Really excited and unable to contain her joy, she pulled a multicolored satiny tunic from the bag. It had elbow-length bell sleeves and a deep V neckline. Riley had changed from his jeans and snap button shirt to a loose-fitting shirt and chinos. His feet were bare and he looked good enough to…undress. The way he was looking at her, he was thinking the same thing about her.

Her throat tightened as dreams about what they might have…might share…wisped around her like the fluffy white clouds in the sky. Giving him a smile that she hoped didn't give away how vulnerable she was feeling, she managed to say, "I'll get changed."

"I'll pour the wine."

She didn't need wine tonight to make her giddy. Just gazing into Riley's eyes made that happen. In her bedroom she quickly pulled out the pins from her chignon and brushed out her hair. After freshening up, dabbing a bit of perfume here and there, she slipped into Riley's gift. She'd seen the tunic at McDougalls and admired it. Riley seemed to know her taste.

When she emerged onto the patio ten minutes later, Riley gave a slow, loud whistle. She felt self conscious again, like a girl on her first date. She'd worn nothing underneath the garment and she knew he could tell.

"And I'm supposed to keep my mind on dinner?" he asked with the lift of a brow.

"That's up to you, I guess." She motioned to their plates. "It looks wonderful."

"Dad's ribs always are. Come on, let's dig in. There's strawberry shortcake for dessert."

"You've thought of everything."

"I certainly hope so."

Picking up her glass, she sipped the wine. "It's good."

He clinked his glass against hers. "To a successful bridal extravaganza. I could tell McDougalls was selling everything like hotcakes, from perfume to pots and pans. I had to stand in line ten deep to get that." He waved at her, but his eyes lingered on the V delving between her breasts, on the silky material sliding over her hips, on her legs, to her bare feet.

They clinked glasses, and miraculously didn't talk about their families. They talked about everything else, from her new clients to the tours he had lined up, to plans for Riley to put a swing set in his backyard. Of course that brought to mind the idea that nothing was going to change, that she'd be going back to New York and he'd be staying here. But for tonight she just let the thought slide through her mind.

When Riley stood after they finished, so did she. He said, "Cuddle up in the lounge chair. I'll light the fire and join you."

What could she say to that? What could she do? Except settle on the chaise and wait for him.

She watched him use a long match to light the kindling. He poked the log on top until it settled into place and caught. Then he closed the screen, leaned the poker against the brick wall and came over to the chair, towering over her.

She slid over and he settled in beside her, wrapping his arm around her. "Are you getting chilly? I can get a cover."

"I don't need a cover with you here."

Those words seemed to be all the incentive he needed. He kissed her until breath was a faraway need, until desire was all that mattered between them, until the thought of tomorrow was pushed far away. Kissing Riley made her happy and excited, and aroused. Touching him did a whole lot more of the same.

He broke their kiss to nuzzle her neck and push the tunic high up her thigh. "You don't have anything on under there," he growled.

"Would you rather I put on more clothes?"

"I'd just have to take them off," he decided, letting his hand wander up even farther. This time when he kissed her, his hunger was inescapable. His tongue did things that caused her fantasies to take flight. This night in itself was a fantasy with the fire going, the darkening sky up above with its half-moon, the twinkling stars that were only this numerous in Miners Bluff. The evergreens around the property, the sage along the wall wafted scents across the patio that made her fantasy real.

Riley made her fantasy real.

"I love it out here with you," she murmured, not saying what she really wanted to say, *I love you*. She didn't know if she was ready to say it out loud. She definitely didn't know if he was ready to hear it—because if sex complicated their parenting, love would do the same. And if it was only one-sided—

Why was trusting so hard for her? Why was believing that she and Riley wanted the same life such a stretch?

Because she was there and he was here. Because their son would have divided loyalties if this didn't work out. Because loving had brought her pain to this point, not fulfillment. Tonight, escaping into Riley seemed to be the only way to prolong happiness. Tonight she could only tell him with her body what she wished she could say with her lips.

His hands grew as possessive as his mouth. Soon she was naked on the chaise, working on the buttons of his shirt, then unfastening his chinos. What they were doing almost seemed forbidden, reckless and impulsive. Yet it also seemed so right. In the confines of the lounge chair, with the scent of pine all around them, Brenna felt transported to that over-the-rainbow place where vows meant something and happily-ever-after was possible.

From somewhere Riley produced a condom and she felt a sudden splash of reality. But then he was gazing into her eyes, asking, "Are you ready?" and she was reaching out to him again. He scooped her leg over his hip and they were as close as two people could be as he slid inside her and held her tight. Their climaxes were a sudden burst of fireworks, lasting longer than any fireworks would. The tremor shook her for a long time, and she could feel Riley shuddering with her. She wanted this union to last forever, and tonight she had hopes that it could.

The following morning was a rush of baby feeding and baby crying and baby swinging. Last night after their time on the patio together, Brenna and Riley had picked up Derek, spent a little time with Shannon, then fed their son and put him to bed. After that they'd crawled into Riley's big bed together and taken up where they'd left off earlier. Now with noon approaching quickly, Derek was in his swing and Riley had gone to the Shamrock to help his dad get ready for tonight. She'd wanted to go, too, but he'd told her he and his dad and his staff could handle it. She should just bring Derek at 4:00 and they'd start the celebration.

She was looking forward to it. She was looking forward to her family and his finally finding peace. Basically last night all they'd done was douse the fire in the outdoor fireplace before driving to Shannon's. So now Brenna brought in the candles from the patio, cooed and gooed at Derek and set his swing in motion again. He loved to be moving. Did that mean he'd like horseback riding? Bike riding? Motorcycle riding? The last she'd rather not think about. She knew watching her son grow as he stretched his wings would cause more than one gray hair. But that was part of having kids and loving them.

Last night Riley had placed the crock from the slow cooker into the sink to soak it overnight. Now Brenna rinsed it, lifted it out and upended it on a towel on the counter. Next she took napkins from the other side of the counter and was about to drop them into the trash when one slipped to the floor. Stooping to retrieve it, she saw something lodged near the molding under the cupboards. It looked like a business card.

Pulling it free, she straightened, turned it in her hand and read it. Walter Turnbull, Attorney At Law, specializing in custody matters. There was an office phone number and a cell phone number.

Brenna's heart fell so far she didn't know if she'd ever find it again. Where had this come from? Had Riley called this man and consulted with him? Had he decided a custody agreement was the way to go? Had he planned that seduction scene last night to wear her down, to convince her to think his way?

She felt heat suffuse her cheeks. She felt her whole body almost vibrate. She wasn't sure what she felt most. Betrayal? Or was she so upset because he'd made a fool of her? He hadn't murmured words of love anytime in the past week *or* last night. They hadn't talked about the future. That's because she'd thought they were finding the road to the future—*their* future. But now she didn't know if Riley would ever be more than a father to Derek. She didn't know if he was planning something behind her back that would make her regret returning to Miners Bluff and telling him he was a dad.

Chapter Twelve

Brenna arrived at the Shamrock Grill and saw that a crowd had already gathered. She'd been hoping to take Riley aside and talk to him about the business card she'd found. But now—

She spotted Shannon and her little boy, and Riley's two brothers, who had changed over the years but not so much that she didn't recognize them. One had his arm around a pretty brunette and two kids seemed to migrate around them. That was Sean. Patrick was near the door to the kitchen, talking to Liam. Around twenty-five other people milled about and she guessed they were friends of Liam's, or Riley and his brothers'. Liam had asked who Brenna might want at the celebration. She had given him Celeste and Clay's names along with Mikala and Dawson, Jenny and Zack, and Katie. All but Katie were seated at one long table, and Brenna's heart warmed that they had come to support her and to celebrate Derek's birth. Katie had told Brenna she'd be a little late.

Riley seemed to appear out of nowhere, smiling, his gaze sending heat waves through her. She remembered everything about last night. She just hoped it hadn't all been a sham.

He took Derek and the car seat from her arms saying, "Over here. Dad has us set up at this long table. Almost everybody came right on time. Do you want hors d'oeuvres?"

Brenna spotted the hors d'oeuvres laid out on the long buffet table. It was definitely more than a veggie tray and dip. She could see warming holders, a fruit tree, as well as small pastries of some kind.

"Your dad went to a lot of trouble."

"Wait until you see the dinner. There are ribs and turkey and all the fixings."

Her hand on Derek's little head, she felt she needed to be grounded. She gazed up at Riley and asked, "Did you help with all of this?"

"Some. Mostly with the restaurant setup. Dad's cook did the rest."

Liam saw her and waved, his expression happy and exuberant.

"I should talk to your dad and thank him."

Just then, the door to the restaurant opened and Angus and Carol McDougall walked in. For a moment a sort of hush ran over the crowd and even Brenna felt as if she took in a long breath and held it.

Then Riley broke the spell. He said to her, "Stay with Derek. I'll bring them over."

In that moment she felt relief and so much love for Riley that she wanted to cry. Could they really do this? Was he going to forget about the past?

Brenna's dad had worn a suit and tie, her mother one of her charity board meeting dresses. They were a little more dressed up than some, but the crowd was varied, from Sunday church clothes to casual. Brenna herself had worn a sundress with a shrug and low pumps. After all, this *was* a celebration.

Her dad looked terrifically uncomfortable until he spotted her, and then he smiled. But when Riley started toward him that smile turned into a cautious expression. She couldn't hear what Riley said to her parents, but after what she expected were a few short hellos, he led them toward the table and everyone else in the room started chattering again. Riley had set the tone and she just hoped it continued.

Her mother hugged her, then bent down to Derek. Her father took her elbow and said, "I have a surprise for you."

"What kind of surprise?" she asked warily.

"Just wait and see. I think you'll like it."

She didn't think today was a good day for surprises but before she could say so, Liam approached the table. Everyone's voices seemed to dim down again.

"Angus," he said.

"Liam," her father returned, his wife watching to see what would happen. But then Angus seemed to blink first. "Thank you for having this party for Derek. Carol brought her camera and we'll take lots of pictures to put in his baby book."

Liam's stance lost some of its tension. "That's a fine idea. I think Riley brought his camera, too. We can trade."

Carol spoke up while motioning to the food. "Everything looks and smells wonderful."

Liam gestured to the head table. "I've seated us

all together. Why don't you fill your plates with hors d'oeuvres and we'll start serving dinner."

Brenna let out that worried breath, but was still concerned about her dad's surprise.

The door opened and closed again and Katie entered the restaurant. When she saw Brenna, she came over to her and Riley. "What a crowd! How do you like the flower arrangements?"

Brenna gazed around and noticed one on the cashier's desk, as well as the individual vases on all of the tables. "You did this?"

"My contribution to the celebration."

Shannon, who had been taking everything in, wandered over from her conversation with her brother, Sean, and touched Katie's arm. "I just love what you've done with the flower shop. It has a fresh look, with that new sign out front and a summer doorstep display. I picked up one of the bouquets on Friday and put it up high where Jakie can't get it. Every time I look at it, it makes me smile."

"That's what flowers are supposed to do," Katie said.

There was movement over by the kitchen doorway and Brenna saw Noah Stone step aside so a server could come through. She noticed when Noah's gaze met Katie's and how it lasted longer than a few moments.

But then Katie looked away and said, "I'm going to check in with Celeste and Jenny and Mikala. I'll talk to you again later." She moved quickly toward the other side of the room, away from Noah.

Brenna hardly had time to think about that because Liam was ushering Patrick and Sean to the table with their family. Patrick gave Brenna a nod, but not a friendly look. Sean looked very serious, glanced at Brenna's dad and then frowned. Her worries started all over again. This wasn't just about her dad and Riley's father. It was about their families, too. She'd wanted to question her dad more about his surprise, but she found herself seated with Riley on one side and Derek on her other. Shannon was in the chair beside Derek's car seat and she gave Derek the attention that a baby deserved.

Brenna said to her, "I'm grateful for you keeping Derek last evening."

"You and Riley deserve some time alone." She gave Brenna a knowing wink. "Everybody in town is talking about the bridal extravaganza at your dad's store. One of my friends is getting married around the holidays and she saw a gown she particularly liked. She said she's going in this week to try it on."

"The gown presentation did seem to go well. If you ever need one—"

"I'm not planning on it anytime soon," Shannon responded with a smile.

Conversation ebbed and flowed as salads were served. Liam was up and about more than in his seat, overseeing everything he could. But he did sit long enough to enjoy dinner, to discuss sports with Angus and Riley, to glance at his sons with a disapproving expression when they didn't join in. After the main course was served, friends and family Brenna didn't know introduced themselves to her and made a fuss over Derek. But he started crying right then, and Brenna knew she should feed and change him before Liam served dessert.

Riley leaned close to her and whispered almost in her ear, "You can go to dad's office if you want to feed him. Do you want me to come along?"

They could talk in Liam's office, but they could also be interrupted at any time. Better if she just changed and fed Derek and came back to the table. She and Riley would have time later to talk.

She stood and gathered up Derek and the diaper bag. "I'm fine. I won't be too long."

She felt Riley's gaze on her back as she threaded her way from the table, then turned left into a short hall that led to Liam's office. She passed the restrooms and a supply room and found the door to the office open. Going inside, she partially closed the door for privacy's sake and for a little quiet for Derek. He ate better when there wasn't a lot of stimulation around him. She knew so much about her son, his preferences and habits, likes and dislikes, without him even being able to talk. Riley seemed to know those same things, but she still couldn't imagine being separated from Derek even for a day.

He ate like the big boy he was becoming. After a burp and a diaper change, she lifted him to her shoulder again and kissed his little forehead. He was growing so fast. She should be taking pictures every day to capture every detail.

She was about to lift the diaper bag from the chair near the door when she heard voices in the hall…almost familiar voices.

Riley?

She was about to step out there when something in the inflection in the tone made her wait. No, it wasn't Riley. Opening the door a little farther, she patted Derek on the back and spotted Sean and Patrick close to the restrooms. Their voices carried to her.

They were engrossed in their discussion and didn't see or hear her.

"I told Riley he should see the lawyer that helped me," Patrick told his brother.

"Riley's smart," Sean responded. "He knows he needs something in black and white."

"Turnbull is good. I wouldn't have the visitation rights that I have if I hadn't hired him. I'm sure he'll call him this week."

Brenna knew she should make a sound, move, let them know she was there. But all of her fears and doubts froze her into place. Rooted to the spot, she could only hold Derek in almost fascinated disappointment.

Patrick's voice was disdainful as he said, "He only took her to bed in high school as payback for what her dad did. It's a shame that when he did it the night of the reunion it backfired."

Riley and his brothers were close. They'd know what he was thinking, wouldn't they? Could it be true? That Riley himself was still bent on revenge? Had he been playing her now to get rights to his son?

She felt sick, almost dizzy, and the last thing she wanted was for Riley's brothers to know she'd overheard. Quietly she stepped back into Liam's office and shut the door. She had to pull herself together and she had to find out the truth. But she couldn't face off with Riley here. She needed privacy for that. Privacy, and a whole lot of courage.

Noah slapped Riley on the back. "It looks as if this is a rousing success. Who would have thought? I was concerned I might have to bring a couple of my officers along with me."

"It's a start," Riley said. "I don't know how I'll get Sean and Patrick to come around. It will probably just take time. Shannon and I will have to wear them down."

Riley caught sight of Brenna coming back into the room. She looked odd—pale, maybe even upset. Her shoulders were back, her chin was up. And were her eyes just a little bit too shiny?

He was about to go to her when Angus McDougall rose to his feet.

Spotting Brenna, too, her father motioned to her chair. "I've been waiting for you, honey. Come on. I have an announcement."

Riley felt a chill of foreboding rush up his spine. Brenna's dad making an announcement at *his* dad's celebration.

Riley put his hand on the back of Brenna's chair to hold it in place while she sat with Derek. But she didn't look at him, and she didn't lean back. She sat as straight as a soldier, and he knew something was wrong. "Brenna?" he asked.

She shook her head. "We have to talk after this," she said, as Angus held up his hand for silence.

Riley was more concerned with Brenna than with Angus. But with Derek pressed against her, she shifted away from him, toward her father.

"It's so good to see everyone here today," Angus said with a broad smile. "I know many of you have children. Having a grandson now, I thought about what he needs and about what the community needs. Our medical center here is top-notch, but it's just a medical center, not a hospital. And sometimes our kids need more than that. I'm going to donate money to Miners Bluff Urgent Care Medical Center to add on a children's wing. It will be a pediatric center so that parents never have to worry about the care of their babies or travel the whole way to Flagstaff. It should be just what the community needs. And with a fundraiser we can have the highest-end medical equipment in it." He looked down at Brenna and Derek. "Only the best for our kids."

As Angus took his seat again, everyone in the room applauded. Riley knew any parent *would* applaud this idea. It was a wonderful gesture, but one that Angus never should have made *here*.

When Riley glanced at his dad, he saw his father's face was turning red. That meant his blood pressure was soaring, and Riley knew why. His father had done everything he could today to make this celebration a wonderful time for all, his expression of his love for his new grandson.

But Angus's grand gesture trumped it in spades.

Now Brenna did look at him, and he saw that she was as astonished as he was.

But he had to ask, "Did you know about this?"

"No, of course I didn't know about this. How could I know?"

Suddenly it was as if everyone in the room were on their feet, many coming over to slap Angus on the back and to talk about his plans.

With dessert finished, guests milled about at will. Jenny, Mikala, Celeste and Katie crossed to Brenna, possibly because they realized what had happened and they wanted to give her their support. But Patrick and Sean were scowling ferociously and Shannon looked as exasperated as he'd ever seen her.

Clay stepped up beside him. "Oh, boy! You never know what's going to happen next, do you? That was a surprise?"

"That was a Roman candle going off in the middle of a dry forest," Riley responded.

Angus had moved away from the table and now Liam went to him and gestured to the back patio.

"Uh-oh," Riley muttered under his breath.

"Maybe it won't be so bad," Clay suggested. "Maybe they'll finally talk everything out."

For one of the first times in his life, Riley didn't know what to do. Should he let the two men have their say?

Brenna shot him a worried glance.

Carol McDougall watched her husband exit the room, trailing behind him and then stopping. It was as if she, too, decided maybe the time for this had come.

The thing was, after a few minutes the voices on the patio grew louder and the chatter in the restaurant grew softer.

Riley knew standing by wasn't an option. As he approached the patio both men were practically shouting.

Liam yelled, "You ruined my marriage!"

Angus yelled back, "You ruined my reputation!"

And then…

All hell broke loose. Riley wasn't sure who took the first swing. Both men seemed to bring up their arms at the same time. He only knew by the time he got there, Angus McDougall's nose was bleeding, there was an angry red mark under his father's eye and the two men looked ready to keep it up all night.

Riley stepped between them and braced a palm on each man's chest. "That's it!" he yelled at them. "That's enough. Do I have to get Noah in here to arrest you for disturbing the peace and disorderly conduct?"

Angus glared at him and so did his father.

"Noah!" Riley called.

The fire seemed to diminish in his father's eyes. He shook his head as he rubbed his eye and stepped away from Riley's bracing hand. Seeing the other man back away, Angus did the same, grabbed a handkerchief from his pocket and held it to his nose. His wife rushed in, but Angus wouldn't let her minister to him.

"You know what?" Riley asked in a stern voice. "Neither of you are fit to be Derek's grandfathers. You're adults and if you don't erase the old scores, none of us are going to be happy. I never want Derek to see this type of behavior and I won't let either of you near him if this is what's going to happen."

A baby's cry broke the deafening silence. Liam, Angus, Carol and Riley turned toward the doorway where Brenna was standing with her son. She didn't look angry as much as disappointed and oh, so sad. He knew how she felt. He turned his back on the two men and crossed to Brenna.

"Come on," he said. "Let's go home."

She cast a concerned glance at her father and mother, but Riley took her elbow and she let him lead her back to their table to pick up their things. Then they exited the restaurant.

They didn't talk on the way back to Riley's house. Brenna seemed shut away in her little world, and he had to admit his thoughts were racing, too. What were they going to do about their families? How were they going to make parenthood work?

He carried Derek's diaper bag into the house, but Brenna didn't seem to want his help. She just said, "Let's talk after I put him to bed." Then she disappeared into her bedroom and he didn't see her again for a good forty-five minutes.

She still looked drawn when she came into the living room where he'd been trying to occupy himself with the sports channel. He switched off the TV. When she didn't sit with him on the sofa, he stood, too.

For some reason, maybe it was the look in her eyes, he became defensive. "Your father didn't have to do that tonight."

At first she seemed taken aback by his attitude. But then she put on what he called Brenna's rebellious face and responded, "He thought he was doing something good. He thought he was doing something for Derek and the other kids in Miners Bluff. Can't you appreciate that?"

"What I can't appreciate is that he stole my father's thunder. This was about my dad doing something nice for us and Derek. Your father couldn't accept that. He had to be the center of attention."

He was ready for Brenna to fight back. He was ready for her to blame his father for giving her dad a bloody nose.

However, she didn't fight back. Rather she stared at him with accusation. "When will this stop, Riley? You said our family's feud doesn't have to affect us, but it does. It affected us when we were teenagers and it's affecting us now. The bad feelings between them have always extended to the two of us."

"What does *that* mean?" He didn't like the defeated tone of her voice or the hurt in her eyes. Where had that come from? In the next moment he knew.

"Did you date me back in high school to get back at my father?"

The way she said it and the emotion behind it, he knew she'd just put her worst doubt and fear into words. His heart actually skipped a beat as he tried to figure out how to handle this. But she must have seen the truth on his face because she turned away.

Riley cupped her elbow. "Brenna, look at me." When she faced him, he knew he had to say it. "That might have been the way it started out."

She looked so betrayed he wanted to pull her into his

arms and never let her go. But she folded her arms across her chest and he knew she wouldn't let him.

"But that's only how it started out," he assured her in a hurry. "Our families weren't on my mind by the end of that summer. They definitely weren't on my mind the night of the reunion."

"How can I ever believe that? How can I ever believe you? I gave you everything I was last night, Riley. Everything. And along with that, I gave you my trust. Today, after you left, I found this on the floor." She produced a business card from her pocket. "That's why I wanted to talk to you when I first arrived at the restaurant."

He stared at the card but didn't take it.

"Are you going to consult a lawyer?"

He hesitated a moment and told her the truth. "Patrick gave me that card because he used this lawyer in his divorce. He said he was good and that we might want an agreement in black and white. But as I told Patrick, I didn't see a reason to call a lawyer as long as you and I could agree on what we wanted."

"Well, Patrick mustn't have thought we agreed, because he told Sean you were going to call Turnbull this week. He also told Sean that in high school you slept with me to get revenge, but that this time when you did it, it was a shame it backfired."

Brenna's gossip dismayed him and he was even more upset that she believed it. "Where did you hear that?"

"I was in your dad's office and Patrick and Sean were in the hall. I could hear them clearly and believe me, I didn't misunderstand what they were saying. I don't know what we have and what we don't have, Riley. I don't know what last night meant or what happened today. I just know I'm really confused and I need to leave. That's what I was doing in there. I was packing. As soon as I have everything together I'll take Derek and go. I won't keep you from him. Just call me and tell me when you want to visit. But I'll be staying with my parents. I can't stay here with you anymore, Riley, I just can't."

She didn't get close enough to let him touch her. She swirled away and disappeared down the hall and into the bedroom quicker than he could go after her. But even if he went after her, he didn't know what he'd say. He couldn't change the past any more than his father or Angus could. And that was *his* downfall, too.

Brenna's mom brought breakfast to her room the following morning. Last night her father and mother had found the cradle they'd used for her when she was a baby. It was handcrafted oak and absolutely beautiful. Her mother had it made up in no time and hadn't tried to have a conversation with Brenna as they'd worked on it.

Last evening Brenna hadn't seemed able to find words to say anything. She'd never felt so horrible or betrayed or downright devastated. When she'd left Riley after high school, she'd loved him and she hadn't wanted to leave. But her better sense had told her they weren't ready and they were too young. They didn't have trust, and might never have it. She'd been right about all of it. But she hadn't wanted to be right. She had hoped Patrick and Sean were so wrong, that Riley had fallen in love with her, and that was all there was to it. But she hadn't been able to escape that shadow of revenge. Maybe if he'd admitted it to her sooner, that that's what he'd done, that that had been his motive—

But Riley's past motivation led her to believe that his

behavior with her and Derek was a manipulation, too. This morning nothing looked any clearer.

The breakfast tray her mom brought didn't entice her to eat.

"Thanks. The tea would have been enough."

Her mom took Derek from her. "You need more than tea. And you need to tell us what happened with Riley. How can we help if—"

Angus suddenly knocked on her bedroom door. "How are you this morning?"

"Not much better than last night," she answered honestly.

He asked her mom, "Would you mind watching Derek for a little while? I'd like to talk to Brenna."

"Of course I don't mind. He's a bundle of joy, for sure. I'll take him outside so he can see all the pretty flowers." Her mother was gone before she could decide if that's what she wanted her to do.

"I'm sorry," Angus said.

Brenna couldn't cover her surprise, but she wasn't sure what he was apologizing for. "What are you sorry about?"

He was dressed for work in a suit, but hadn't yet added a tie to his open shirt collar. He went over to the queen-size canopy bed and sat on it looking ridiculous, with the ruffles brushing his trousers and those same ruffles above his head. "I'm sorry for everything about yesterday. I should have been a guest who kept my mouth shut. I never should have brought up the medical center."

"Not there," she agreed. "Not after Liam had gone to so much trouble to give us what *he* could give us. You just trampled his present, Dad."

"Yeah, I can see it looked that way. And I never meant to start a fistfight. You've got to believe that."

"I believe you didn't mean to start it, but it happened anyway. And now—" Her voice caught and Angus heard it.

"Ah, Brenna. I'm so sorry this didn't work out, because you and Riley—" He stopped. "You have IT."

Her astonishment made her blurt out, "We have IT?"

"Don't tell me you don't know what I mean. And don't make me have this conversation with you. I don't want to get into the whys and wherefores of why you two migrate toward each other."

"Migrate?"

"What else would you call it?" He held up his hand. "No, don't tell me."

She almost smiled. Almost.

"You're unhappy here without him," he concluded.

"I've only been here one night, Dad. How can you tell?"

"Baby, all I have to do is look into your eyes and I can tell. Whether you believe it or not, I know you. I've always known you. And from that day you almost drowned, I considered protecting you to be my life's work. You didn't seem to mind too much at first. You didn't seem to mind until Riley came into the picture."

"You didn't know Riley was *in* the picture."

"Do you think I'm deaf, dumb and blind? My precious only daughter looked at Riley O'Rourke as if he was a teen idol. I could see that. I knew when you were late there was a reason. I had my security guard follow you one day."

"Oh, Daddy."

"Yeah, it might have been wrong. And was I never more relieved and pleased at the end of that summer when you decided to go to New York, getting you away from him, I thought. Even if it meant you were so far away."

"You never said anything."

"Of course not. You thought you had a secret. I didn't think this was a secret that would blow up in your face. But it did, fifteen years later."

She went over to the dresser, pulled open a drawer that had a few of her things in it, then shut it again. "I'm not going to stay in Miners Bluff any longer, Dad. I know you can handle the bridal extravaganza on your own. I need to go back to New York."

"Last time you left Miners Bluff you were heading toward something. This time, I think you're just running. Do you think you'll be any happier when you get to New York?"

She turned to face her father. "What am I supposed to do? I love Riley. But I don't think he feels anything for me. I think he just wants access to his son."

Angus's brows went up.

"Yes, we have chemistry. We always did and we always will. But that's not what love is made of. That's not what trust is made of."

"You're so sure what Riley feels?"

"No, I'm *not* sure at all. And he's not saying. I feel used, all the way around. He used me to get back at you when we were dating in high school, and he used me again after the reunion. After I came back here, maybe he seduced me again on purpose to make sure I'd give him plenty of time with Derek. The thing is, Dad, he didn't have to do that. I've always loved Riley. He could have had as much time as he wanted with his son. We could have worked it out. Now I don't know what we're going to do."

Angus stood, went to his daughter and dropped his arm around her shoulders. "You'll figure it out. You always do."

But Brenna didn't feel as if she was going to figure out anything. Not before it was too late.

Chapter Thirteen

Riley took a firm grip on the ax a few days later and brought it down smartly on the log, splitting it in two. He heard a truck's crunch of tires on gravel on his driveway. He also knew exactly who that truck belonged to. He positioned another log on the stump, raised the ax, took aim and brought it down forcefully again. He felt his dad's presence before he heard his voice.

"Is that helping?" his father asked.

The sun was just slipping behind the horizon, but there was still enough heat in the day to make physical labor sweaty. He knew he probably looked as bad as he felt, with his T-shirt dark with perspiration and his beard stubble growing heavier with each passing day. He remained silent, though he did glance over his shoulder at his father.

"Are you still angry at me for starting that fight with Angus?"

"What good would it do if I was?"

"Point taken," Liam said. "I think we should talk."

"There's nothing to talk about."

"Oh, I think there is. Plenty. Have you seen Brenna since she moved out of your place?"

Shannon had called him after the disaster at the Shamrock and he'd told her Brenna had gone to stay with her parents. That really had said it all. "No, I haven't seen her or talked to her."

"Why?"

"Because she doesn't want to see or talk to me. I *am* going to see Derek, though. But I thought I'd give it a few days."

"I closed down my heart after your mother left and kept it closed down all these years. That makes for a very lonely life."

If his dad had wanted his attention, he got it now. "You drank because you were lonely? You had all of us around!"

"I drank because your mother didn't want me or the life I wanted to give her. And yes, I was lonely for her, even when you kids were around. But even when I got sober, I was still lonely. Granted, not for her anymore. But a woman fills a man's loneliness the way nobody else can. I just didn't want to take the risk again."

"Why are you telling me this?"

"Because I don't want you to make the same mistake."

A mockingbird called as a swallow swooped toward the tall grass.

"I'm not drinking," Riley said tersely.

"No, but I know you. You'll bury yourself in guiding jobs or split logs till you drop. I think you need to face a little reality."

"And that is?"

"Brenna didn't fall in love with another man. She didn't turn her back on you because you couldn't get back on your feet."

"No, she turned her back on me because I first dated her out of a need for revenge. She turned her back on me because she thought I didn't trust her."

"Did you?"

Riley thought about the DNA test, holding onto that lawyer's card. Why hadn't he thrown it away? Brenna had never been anything but honest with him. She'd brought Derek to him so he *could* have a relationship with his son. As she'd said, she'd given him everything she was. And yet, still, that tiny bit of doubt had remained. Why? Because he wasn't exactly sure how she felt about him? Or because he didn't want to be the vulnerable one and admit how *he* felt about *her?*

"I don't know how to fix this, Dad."

"Do you love her?"

"Yes," he said, feeling as if the breath had been knocked out of him with the confession.

"Then fixing this shouldn't be so hard. You just have to convince her you *do* love her. Maybe you might even have to get Angus on board to help."

"Her father?"

"Isn't it the proper thing to do? To ask a man's permission before you ask for his daughter's hand in marriage?"

Of course, that *was* the proper thing to do.

As Riley stood at Starfall Point on Moonshadow Mountain two days later, he heard the women's voices before he saw them. He'd enlisted Mikala, Celeste, Jenny and Katie's help, as well as Angus's. Brenna's father had taken Riley's call, which had been his first surprise. He'd been all set to keep calling, one way or the other until he got through to the man. Angus's hello had been stern when Riley had phoned the store and gone through the receptionist. But Riley was used to stern. Before Brenna's father could hang up on him, he'd told Angus his plan, asking Angus to help urge Brenna out of the house, to encourage her to go on an afternoon of hiking with her friends. Then he'd told Angus why.

Angus had asked, "And if I do this, if I help *you* do this, what guarantee do I have that you're going to make her happy?"

Riley had been honest. "I can't give you a guarantee, sir. There aren't any. But I can tell you I'll be the best husband I know how to be to Brenna, and the best father I can be to Derek."

"And the difficulties between our families?"

"Maybe you'll have to make a guarantee to me that *you'll* do everything in your power to change that."

Riley had ended that call knowing he and Angus McDougall understood each other.

He wanted to run down the trail and meet Brenna. But he didn't. He stayed where he was. Soon the women came into view, walking through the purple wild geraniums and golden columbine and high grass, talking and laughing.

Then there she was, and there he was and they were gazing into each other's eyes again.

"Riley, what are you doing here?"

"I asked your friends to bring you here so I could talk to you. Thank you," he said to the women.

Mikala patted Brenna's arm. "We'll see you later."

Looking panicked, Brenna asked, "Mikala, where are you going?"

Celeste gave her a smile. "You and Riley need to talk. We'll be around if you need us later."

After Jenny and Katie gave Riley thumbs-up signs, all of the women headed down the trail and Brenna stood perfectly still.

He approached her. "They're not deserting you. They're just giving you over to my safekeeping."

She didn't look as if she believed that. If only he could do this right. If only she believed what he had to say.

He took her hand.

She resisted for a moment, but then seemed to decide that wasn't the best course. Her blond hair blew in the sudden breeze. As his gaze passed down her beaded T-shirt and her well-worn jeans and boots, he knew she'd never looked prettier and he'd never desired her more. His fingers folded around her hand and he led her to Starfall Point, where the valley below and the town of Miners Bluff spread before them.

"I have something for you," he said.

She looked puzzled when he pulled an envelope from his cargo pants pocket and buttoned it again. He handed it to her.

"Riley, if this is some kind of agreement about Derek—"

He cut her off by gently placing his finger over her lips. "Open it," he urged her.

She pulled out the sheet of paper, glanced at it and then back at him. "This is an airline confirmation of three one-way tickets to New York."

"Yes, it is. When I came back to Miners Bluff and settled in again, I thought I needed lots of land around me and the freedom to do what I wanted when I wanted to. After the night of the reunion you were constantly on my mind *and* in my heart, even though I didn't want to admit it. After all, it was an old habit I'd perfected fighting feelings for you. I'd been doing it since we were teenagers. I've been looking for the wrong things in the wrong places just like I did when I was a teenager. I was hot for you in high school. Yes, I first dated you in defiance of our families and possibly to get revenge. But once we got to know each other, I felt so much I didn't know how to handle it. When you wouldn't let me take our relationship public, I felt betrayed. But my feelings for you never went away. That's why the night of the reunion happened. I didn't have the past on my mind that night, just chemistry."

"Riley—"

"You've got to let me finish, because I may never get this out again. I made some calls yesterday. There's more than one firm in New York interested in my services. I can go back into IT consulting until we figure out exactly where we want to live and whether or not I want to start some kind of guiding service in New York or Connecticut."

"But you don't like big cities."

"We could live in Connecticut. I hear there are trees and flowers and even deer there. We can work out all that. The important thing is that the three of us build a life together."

This time he reached into his shirt pocket and he slid out a ring. The antique setting with its multitude of diamonds would remind them of the years they'd loved each other, the love that had taken root long ago but had grown and matured. He didn't hesitate to drop down onto one knee.

Brenna put her hand to her mouth but he captured it again. "Brenna McDougall, I love you with all my heart. That love has grown over the years and I know it's going to get bigger than anything we can predict. Our love is going to make our lives rich and full and give Derek the start he needs for his life to be the same. I loved you long before he came along. I want to marry you because of that love. Will you be my wife?"

Brenna's tears started to flow then. She let go of the airline confirmation to put one hand on either side of his face. Then she knelt down with him in the soft grass in the middle of wildflowers and the scent of pine and said, "I love you, Riley O'Rourke. Yes, I'll marry you."

As the airline reservation fluttered in the breeze and fell down into the valley below, their kiss seemed to go on forever.

And that's exactly what Riley wanted...forever.

Epilogue

Brenna watched Riley lift Derek high in the air as they stood in front of the gazebo in Miners Bluff historic park. Ever since Riley had asked her to marry him, she'd been floating on air, designing more creatively than she ever had, including Aunt Anna's wedding gown, caring for Derek with so much love she knew she could handle anything. That afternoon on Starfall Point she'd seen the honesty, vulnerability and overwhelming love in Riley's eyes. It was what she'd wanted to see for a very long time. She'd moved back into his house again and they were thinking about an October wedding. Tomorrow they'd be flying back to New York to make some decisions there.

Maybe every summer they could return to Miners Bluff to spend more time with their families, in addition to other times throughout the year when they could both get away. They had so many plans to make, and a lifetime to make them. But the wedding was uppermost in her mind now, and how they were going to make arrangements both families could live with.

"Your father didn't say why he wanted to meet us here?" she asked Riley as he cuddled Derek into the crook of his arm and held him comfortably.

"Nope. He just said he wanted to talk to us here at the gazebo."

They heard footsteps on the path leading to the gazebo and when they turned to see if it was Liam, Brenna spotted her dad, too. The two men were approaching them together.

"Oh, my gosh! I think the world's going to tilt on its axis," she murmured.

"It already did that the day I met you," Riley teased, as he slung his arm around her and held her close. It was the three of them against the world. She just hoped it wasn't going to be the three of them against their dads.

After hugs all around, Riley asked, "All right, so what's this about?"

The two men exchanged a look. Then Liam said, "Don't think we're the best of friends. We're not. We're tolerating each other. But we decided to work on something for you. I just happen to know the mayor. I went to school with Everett and he comes into the restaurant once a week with his wife. We've struck up a friendship again. Anyway, because of that, he said he will give the two of you permission to get married in the gazebo and to have your reception in the park."

Angus cleared his throat. "We thought this location would be neutral, and we could have as many people as we wanted. Since Liam pulled the strings to make this happen, I offered to take care of the canopies and the flowers. He's going to handle the food. What do you think?"

She and Riley had been exploring all the options. They hadn't particularly wanted to have a luxurious wedding, just one where all their friends and family could celebrate with them. This actually sounded like the perfect idea.

She looked up at Riley. "What do you think?"

"I kind of like the idea. What about you?"

"I kind of like it, too."

"We should stick to the beginning of October," Liam said, "so the weather holds."

"How long did it take for the two of you to come up with this plan?" Brenna asked teasingly.

"Not very long."

"Who made the first call?" Riley asked, and Brenna knew he wanted everything out in the open with no secrets and full disclosure.

"Actually, Brenna's mother did," Angus admitted. "Women seem to be better at reconciliation than men."

"Though I *have* talked to Patrick and Sean," Liam assured them. "They say they'll behave. They say they'll keep an open mind. We all need some time to settle in. But we will, because we all love you."

Brenna felt tears come to her eyes again. She'd been doing a lot of that happy crying. When she did, Riley just held her, like he was now.

Derek made a happy baby sound.

Liam asked, "May I?"

Riley handed his son over to his grandfather.

Angus told them, "We'll take a walk and give you a couple of minutes to discuss things. Then you can tell us what you really think," he added with a grin. He and

Liam started off with their grandson under the shade of the live oaks in the summer sun.

"We don't need to talk, do we?" Riley asked her.

"Nope. I like the plan."

He pulled her up the couple of steps into the privacy of the gazebo. "Well, good. Then we can make out until they come back."

He took her in his arms and kissed her. She returned his passion and his promise, knowing happily-ever-after wasn't far away.

* * * * *

COMING NEXT MONTH from Harlequin® Special Edition®

AVAILABLE AUGUST 21, 2012

#2209 THE PRODIGAL COWBOY

Kathleen Eagle

Working with Ethan is more challenging than investigative reporter Bella ever dreamed. He's as irresistible as ever, and he has his own buried secrets.

#2210 REAL VINTAGE MAVERICK

Montana Mavericks: Back in the Saddle

Marie Ferrarella

A widowed rancher has given up on love—until he meets a shop owner who believes in second chances. Can she get the cowboy to see it for himself?

#2211 THE DOCTOR'S DO-OVER

Summer Sisters

Karen Templeton

As a kid, he would have done anything to make her happy, to keep her safe. As an adult, is he enough of a man to let her do the same for him?

#2212 THE COWBOY'S FAMILY PLAN

Brighton Valley Babies

Judy Duarte

A doctor and aspiring mother agrees to help a cowboy looking for a surrogate—and falls in love with him.

#2213 THE DOCTOR'S CALLING

Men of the West

Stella Bagwell

Veterinary assistant Laurel Stanton must decide if she should follow her boss and hang on to a hopeless love for him...or move on to a new life.

#2214 TEXAS WEDDING

Celebrations, Inc.

Nancy Robards Thompson

When she opens her own catering company,
AJ Sherwood-Antonelli's professional dreams are finally coming true. The last thing she needs is to fall for a hunky soldier who doesn't want to stay in one place long enough put down roots....

Enjoy an exclusive excerpt
from Harlequin® Special Edition®
THE DOCTOR'S DO-OVER by Karen Templeton

"What I actually said was that this doesn't make sense."

She cocked her head, frowning. "This?"

His eyes once again met hers. And held on tight.

Oh. This. Got it.

Except…she didn't.

Then he reached over to palm her jaw, making her breath catch and her heart trip an instant before he kissed her. Kissed her good. And hard. But good. Oh, so good, his tongue teasing hers in a way that made everything snap into focus and melt at the same time— Then he backed away, hand still on jaw, eyes still boring into hers. Tortured, what-the-heck-am-I-doing eyes. "If things had gone like I planned, this would've been where I dropped you off, said something about, yeah, I had a nice time, too, I'll call you, and driven away with no intention whatsoever of calling you—"

"With or without the kiss?"

"That kiss? Without."

O-kaay. "Noted. Except…you wouldn't do that."

His brow knotted. "Do what?"

"Tell me you'll call if you're not gonna. Because that is not how you roll, Patrick Shaughnessy."

He let go to let his head drop back against the headrest, emitting a short, rough laugh. "You're going to be the death of me."

"Not intentionally," she said, and he laughed again. But it was such a sad laugh tears sprang to April's eyes.

"No, tonight did not go as planned," he said. "In any way, shape, form or fashion. But weirdly enough in some ways it went better." Another humorless laugh. "Or would have, if you'd been a normal woman."

"As in, whiny and pouty."

"As in, not somebody who'd still be sitting here after what happened. Who would've been out of this truck before I'd even put it in Park. But here you are..." In the dim light, she saw his eyes glisten a moment before he turned, slamming his hand against the steering wheel.

"I don't want this, April! Don't want...you inside my head, seeing how messy it is in there! Don't want..."

He stopped, breathing hard, and April could practically hear him think, *Don't want my heart broken again.*

***

Look for
THE DOCTOR'S DO-OVER
by Karen Templeton
this September 2012 from Harlequin® Special Edition®.

HSEEXP0912